Manifest Secrets

Books by Dale E. Lehman

Howard County Mysteries

The Fibonacci Murders

True Death

Ice on the Bay

A Day for Bones

Bernard and Melody Capers

Weasel Words

Rooftop Sonata

Science Fiction

Space Operatic

The Belt

Penitence

Short Story Collections

The Realm of Tiny Giants

Found by the Road

Manifest Secrets

MANIFEST SECRETS

stories by

DALE E. LEHMAN

RED TALES

Chase, Maryland

Manifest Secrets
Dale E. Lehman

Cover art by Proi

Book design by Dale E. Lehman
Book set in 11-pt. Le Monde Livre Classique

Published by Red Tales, 2023
Baltimore, Maryland
United States of America
https://www.DaleELehman.com

Trade paperback: 978-1-958906-06-4
Ebook: 978-1-958906-07-1

Dedication

For Gabriel, a spirit unsubdued.

No AI tools were used in the crafting of this story. Seriously, where would be the fun in *that*?

THE STORIES

Introduction

Something happened on the way to this collection. *The Realm of Tiny Giants* and *Found by the Road* charted a course from flash fiction contests to Medium.com publications, with a few side trips. *Manifest Secrets* turns those side trips into major destinations.

One such destination: the NYC Midnight short story competitions. No less than five of these tales—"The Foretelling," "Keep Out Signs," "Worstseller," "Seth," and "Hot Ice"—were written for them. "The Foretelling" and "Hot Ice" placed in the top five of my sections. The others, although not garnering such honors, all received significant praise from the judges. I think you'll enjoy them all. And "Seth" is a special story to me, based in Lehman family history.

A second destination arose from an invitation to lead a creative writing workshop in February, 2022 at Maryland Institute College of Arts. The workshop was an outreach event in conjunction with an art exhibition curated and presented by students in MICA's Exhibition Development Seminar. We used art from their exhibition as writing prompts. At that time, I was focused on finishing my novel *A Day for Bones*. Short stories being off my radar, I prepared with literary stretches using prompts from the Art Institute of Chicago's website. The result was a unique set of short stories, most of which are included here: "Beta Read," "Stick Men," "Five," "The Memory Bag," "The Jukebox," and "Taxman." For the workshop, I wrote a story based on artist Leo Sewell's sculpture "Grasshopper." (Another of his sculptures was in the exhibition. "Grasshopper," alas, was not.) That story bears my favorite title from this collection: "Do Steampunk Orthopterans Swim?"

Not every destination worked out. "The Fisherman that Got Away" and "Unstuck," were the start of a planned series on Medium called "Too Tall Tales." Unfortunately, after three stories (one of which was too weak to include here), the series stalled. Oh, well. Still, those two make a fun pair.

As before, there are side-trips here, too, stories that came to me out of the blue. Most I'll just let you read, but I'd like to call out three.

First: "The Sculpture" was inspired by "The Temptation of Harringay" by H. G. Wells, which I discovered in one of my father's old science fiction books. In Wells' story, a figure painted by a mediocre artist comes to life and offers the artist the ability to create masterpieces in exchange for his soul. It was such a good story that my mind seized upon it and twisted it into something…different. As they say, imitation is the sincerest form of flattery!

Second: "Miraculous Morgan," which began with alliteration. I noticed that Morgan is both a first and last name, so I created a woman named Morgan Morgan and dropped her in Miami. And made her magical. Well, miraculous, actually, to avoid a legal issue. (Turns out, Magic Morgan is a real-life professional magician, although he's a he.) True, there must be many Morgans in Miami, but that's okay. My Morgan is unique. When you meet her, you'll see.

And third, the most moving moment of this journey, "Chicory." "Chicory" isn't a story but a poem, the only poem I've written since high school. Looking out my front door on Father's Day 2023, I spotted some chicory blooming pale blue at the edge of the road. Kathleen often said our anniversary was approaching when the chicory bloomed. She first noticed this in June 1977, shortly before our wedding. She passed away June 27, 2022, one week after our 45th anniversary. Seeing those flowers three days before our 46th, it felt as though she'd planted them for me.

And so, the poem spilled out.

The Foretelling

"It's a fraud, Magnolia." Heather's words blew across the group of girls on the common, a cold wind chasing off the high summer heat. "It's for little kids, not for adults."

Magnolia blushed. She turned twelve a week from today, leaving childhood behind. Henceforth, she would be a woman. Her mother had come to town to purchase supplies for the celebration while Magnolia issued personal invitations to friends and important acquaintances. A dozen girls, mostly younger than she, crowded around, inquiring, speculating, teasing. She felt dizzy. Her quiet voice got lost in the din.

And then Heather arrived and took charge, as always. Now fourteen, she set her hands to her hips the way mothers did when scolding. With long, golden curls and more figure than the others, she radiated authority. "At my Foretelling, we expected something special. I'll be mayor someday, after all. But—"

"Girls can't be mayor!" Violet objected. Only ten, Violet was the daughter of a moneylender, the richest man in the town. Like her father, she feared no one, not even Heather.

Heather looked down her nose at Violet. "If girls can be queen, they can be mayor."

Violet pouted while Heather turned back to Magnolia.

A slight child, Magnolia felt even smaller under Heather's gaze. Her father wasn't rich like Violet's, wasn't an influential merchant like Heather's. He was a farmer, honest and hard-working but as lowly as the land. Magnolia's passage to womanhood wouldn't be marked by the lavish celebration Heather had received. Family, friends, and food, yes, but country-fashion. No fawning town elders, no paid musicians, no elaborate confections. There would be but one similarity.

The Foretelling.

As evening crept over the land and the guests dispersed, the Toymaker would arrive to test Magnolia and bestow a gift that was outwardly a toy but inwardly a portent. Magnolia would shrink under the old woman's gaze even as she shrank under Heather's. To children, the Toymaker was a generous fairy, showering them with gifts and laughter, but in the Foretelling she became witch and augur. She looked into your soul and charted your destiny. She had done so for centuries. Magnolia didn't know how the Toymaker could be so ancient, but that's what everyone said.

Heather resumed her theme. "She gave *me* a doll. A stupid, ordinary doll. It wasn't magic. It didn't even look clever. I was so mad, I called her a hideous hag. She couldn't do a thing about it, either, because Father was standing right there, and he thought so, too. He was as angry as I."

The girls all sucked in their breaths. Magnolia thought Heather foolish to speak to the Toymaker so. She, certainly, would never do such a thing. But then, she couldn't even ask Heather what the doll meant. It must have meant something.

"Don't hope for much, Magnolia," Heather said. "You're destined to marry a farmer. You don't need the Toymaker to tell you that." She laughed. "But if she gives you a pitchfork, jab her for me."

Magnolia looked at her feet. "I couldn't," she said. If only she had Heather's strength, Heather's boldness, the Toymaker wouldn't dare humiliate her.

Heather gave her a look of pity. "Probably not," she said. "Just remember, whatever that beldam says is a lie. Don't let her fool you."

Heather's prediction stuck with Magnolia for days. She had never thought much about the future. She knew only the farm, her chores, the crops, the animals. Her mother taught her to cook and sew, and her father taught her planting and harvesting and haying. From her older brother Cypress, she learned names of birds and footprints of rabbits, foxes and more. Marriage and children always seemed distant. Yet she supposed Heather was right. Heather was fourteen, after all, and knew so much of the world. She was clever and strong and might indeed be mayor someday. But for Magnolia, someday looked much like the past.

Two days before her birthday, Magnolia was helping fill apple, cherry, and mince pies and pinch the crusts when she wondered what the Foretelling had been like for her mother. Strange to think, Mother had once been a girl, had once turned twelve and stood before the Toymaker. Almost before she knew she was doing it, she asked about it.

Mother checked the oven and came to the table. She brushed a splash of flour from the edge and smiled. "I was scared stiff. But it wasn't half as bad as I feared. Most things aren't."

"What did the Toymaker give you?"

"A set of blocks."

"Just blocks?"

"Just blocks."

"Why?"

Mother picked up the cherry pie and slid it into the oven. Returning to the table, she pushed the other two close together. "These look very much alike, don't they? But on the inside, they're different."

Pointing, Magnolia said, "That's apple, that's mince."

"You made them. But before they're cut, how will our guests know which is which?"

"By smell."

"You can't see into a person's heart and mind. Sometimes you don't even know your own heart or mind. But there are signs. The Toymaker reads them and gives a gift that helps you know yourself."

"Heather said she got an ordinary doll. She said the Toymaker's a fraud."

Mother brushed her hands on her apron and tousled Magnolia's hair. "Heather thinks she knows everything. She never looked inside herself."

Magnolia didn't think that answered anything. "What did the blocks mean?"

"What do you do with blocks?"

"Build."

"There you go."

"What did you build with them?"

"My life." When Magnolia scrunched up her face in confusion and not a little disgust, Mother laughed. "You wouldn't understand. You didn't know me when I was twelve, and it would take too long to tell. Let's just say the Toymaker gave me a push in the right direction."

It must be an adult thing. After she turned twelve and was an adult herself, maybe then Magnolia would understand. She supposed she could wait two more days.

"They weren't ordinary blocks," Mother added. "They glowed sometimes, like a rainbow."

Magnolia gasped. "They were magic blocks?"

"I guess. They only ever glowed for me, when nobody was around."

"Why?"

"Now, how would I know that?" Mother got a faraway look and stared out the window. "In fact, they only glowed when I forgot about them."

"I know!" Magnolia said, suddenly excited. "So you wouldn't forget what they meant!"

"Clever young lady, aren't you?" Mother winked at her, and Magnolia felt she had just passed a test.

Her day came. After breakfast, Mother presented Magnolia with a handmade white cotton dress embroidered with roses. Putting it on, Magnolia gaped at her image in her full-length mirror. She never imagined she could look so beautiful. Outside, her father led a cadre of uncles and cousins pitching a great tent and setting up tables and chairs while her mother and aunts prepared the food.

The guests flowed in at midday. Talk and laughter filled the air. People sure could be noisy! Magnolia circulated among them with a glazed smile on her lips. Adults congratulated, cousins and friends teased. Cypress pointed out all the eligible young bachelors in attendance and ranked their suitability as husbands for her.

Midafternoon, a storm blew in, and in a rush everyone shunted food and dishes inside. The house could barely contain the throng. Magnolia slipped to the side of the living room and stared out the window at the waves of rain. The house grew hot and noise throbbed in her head.

Her father came to her side and put his arm about her shoulders. "Why the long face?"

She shrugged.

"This won't last. Once it blows over, we'll go outside again."

"How do you know?"

"Magic."

Magnolia smiled at his teasing, but she wished the day would just end. She'd collected good wishes and blessings from everyone. Now food and talk consumed them, and she had been forgotten.

"It'll be over before you know it," Father said. "I was sick of my twelfth birthday as soon as the first guest arrived." He nudged her. "Know what your grandfather used to say?"

Magnolia shook her head.

"Glad to see company come, glad to see company go."

She laughed a little, but the guests were only the half of it. "There's the Foretelling still."

"There is that. But at least that will be quiet."

"What did the Toymaker give you?"

He took her hand. "Come on, I'll show you." Worming their way through the crowd, he led her into the back of the house to the mudroom, where he pointed to a storm glass mounted on the wall. A plain glass tube three quarters filled with clear liquid, it was backed by a square of dark wood. It had hung there all Magnolia's life, so she seldom noticed it. Now, as she watched, the liquid turned pale green.

"See? Everything will be fine now." Father pointed out the window. The rain had stopped. Rainbows flashed in the droplets dripping from the trees as they caught fleeting rays of sunshine peeking through the dispersing clouds.

Something in his voice told Magnolia he meant more than the weather. "Does it tell the future?"

"Not exactly."

She thought for a moment. "It tells you if you're going the right way."

"Brains were never your problem," he said with an impish grin.

"What is my problem?"

Mother appeared in the doorway. "Come on, you two. We're moving back outside. Help me get this mob out of my kitchen."

Father motioned Magnolia forward. "Mind those white shoes," he said. "It'll be muddy out there."

Afternoon gave way to evening. The food was reduced to crumbs. People began to take their leave, and gradually a measure of quiet returned to the farm. Magnolia collapsed in a chair under the tent and watched the near-full moon rise in the east. Of a sudden, the few remaining guests rushed through hasty farewells and vanished. Wondering why, Magnolia watched them go. Against the flow, a dark figure picked its way up the lane toward the house.

Mother came to Magnolia's side and whispered, "It's time."

Magnolia rose, trembling. She could scarce breathe as the figure drew near and nearer until it resolved into an old woman with silver hair and hands as wrinkled as dried fruit. Wearing an unremarkable green dress, she stopped a pace away and looked into Magnolia's eyes with an intensity hard to meet. Magnolia did her best not to shrink though she wanted to hide.

"Please," Mother said, "sit. Rest."

"Thank you," the Toymaker said, "but I'm not tired. Not tonight." She fluttered her hand to dismiss her hostess. With a quick glance at Magnolia, Mother withdrew to the house. A moment later, she and her husband looked out the kitchen window, apprehensive.

"You need privacy," the Toymaker said. "Let's walk." She hooked her arm through Magnolia's, and they walked side-by-side down the lane toward the fields. The ground was wet from the rain, and Magnolia's white shoes gathered up mud.

"Ask me something," the Toymaker said once they were out of sight of the house.

Magnolia knew she was to be tested. Was this it? What if she asked the wrong question, a stupid question, a question offensive to the Toymaker?

The Toymaker put up a hand and stopped. She cocked her head as though listening for something in the field. "No," she finally said. "There are no wrong questions. Go on. Ask me something."

A hundred questions flooded Magnolia's mind. Who was this woman? Was she really as old as people said? Why was it hers to usher children through the door to adulthood? Could she really do magic?

But when she finally spoke, it wasn't a deep question, wasn't a question any sensible person would have asked.

"What's your name?"

The Toymaker laughed. She had a laugh like the ringing of bells or the rising of the sun. "You know, I've quite forgotten! Nobody's called me by name for such a long time."

Magnolia thought that sad.

The Toymaker leaned to Magnolia's ear and whispered, "Call me Lily." She straightened and nodded. "Go on, give it a try."

It seemed impertinent, but she'd been invited, so she said, "Hello, Lily."

"Hello, Magnolia. Ask me another question." They began to walk again.

"What's it like, being grown up?"

"Very good. That's a question almost nobody asks. Not even grownups ask it very often. It will be hard, Magnolia, but not without its rewards. Ask another."

"Will Heather be mayor someday?"

"Does it matter?"

Magnolia tried to imagine Heather as mayor. She couldn't. She knew nothing about running a town, so she couldn't imagine the difference Heather might make. Certainly, Magnolia's life wouldn't change much out here on the farm. "I guess not," she said. "Except maybe to Heather."

Lily laughed.

Emboldened, Magnolia asked another question, and another, and another, questions about being a woman and marriage and far-off towns and kings and queens and the stars overhead. She felt a thrill of amazement at her newfound courage here in the gathering dark with just the two of them speaking of such things. The Toymaker never uttered more than a sentence in answer, but it seemed to Magnolia her words both unraveled and deepened the mystery of the world.

As they spoke, Lily steered them back toward the house. They approached the golden lights shining from the windows and came to the front porch. The Toymaker reached into a deep pocket at her hip and drew something out. She presented it to Magnolia as though giving a gift of gold to a queen. "For you, young woman."

Magnolia held it up in the light shining through the front door window. It was a doll, a rather plain-looking rag doll with hair the color of Magnolia's and an unsmiling mouth. She imagined Heather's doll had been much the same. She felt a vague disappointment, but she didn't believe the Toymaker gave idle gifts. "What does it mean?" she asked.

"What do you think it means?"

"Heather said..."

"Shhh." Lily touched a finger to Magnolia's lips. "Heather must walk her path. You must walk yours. Now tell me. What do you think it means?"

Magnolia considered the doll again. It was so plain, it could be anyone she might imagine. "I think it means possibility."

Lily touched a finger to the doll's hair, then touched Magnolia's. "Clearly, I needn't tell you to be clever," she said. "But never be afraid." Without warning, she became shadow and flew like a hawk into the night.

Magnolia smiled after her and hugged her doll. When she looked at it again, the doll was smiling, too.

Keep Out Signs

A light chop danced over the face of the Chesapeake. Wave peaks sparkled in the morning sun while darkness swirled in the troughs like entrances to the underworld. At the helm of his cargo boat, Chuck Boyd amused himself with that image. Water postmen, unlike their land-bound colleagues, both delivered and hauled away, carrying mail and supplies to isolated islanders, returning with trash and sometimes the deceased bound for the Port of Havre de Grace. It was a long slog, and body disposal—although not an everyday occurrence—entailed forms and fees and registered transport coffins. If only they could dump the departed into the bay.

Rounding Love Point, Boyd bore east-southeast toward the Kent Narrows Archipelago, a weird name for a wide swath of water dotted with islands. Kent Narrows vanished twenty years ago as rising sea levels and sinking bedrock fragmented the land. In another half century, only flecks of rock and mud would remain. Maybe when the last landowners fled, mapmakers would change it. For now, people held as stubbornly to the name as they did their ephemeral ground.

In the meantime, Boyd's boat bobbing over the water was a welcome sight to islanders. He cultivated cordial relations with those on his route, not because it lifted their spirits, although it probably did, but because they were strange and desperate folk prone to fits of insanity. There were stories. Postmen on well-maintained craft had vanished among the islands in perfect weather. Boyd loved the freedom of his boat and the smell of the bay, but he had no illusions about the people he served.

He took it at a moderate clip and in fifteen minutes made Boot Island, a sliver of land five hundred feet long shaped like a pointy-toed boot. Just two people called this island home: a skeletal old white man named Dr. Mezick, a long-retired physician who held claim to the leg of the island, the larger stretch to the north; and a brown-skinned woman of thirty-seven who called herself Chastity although she wasn't chaste, not when Boyd came to call. She owned the foot of the island. A rickety white picket fence crossing the boot's narrow ankle separated their holdings. Mezick was Boyd's first stop, Chastity his favorite. The two neighbors, for their part, hated each other.

Mezick never failed to bring that up, usually sooner rather than later. This time it was the first thing from mouth. "You ain't seein' that whore again, I hope. You oughta stay away from her. She'll stab you in the back and steal your boat, like she stole my land. Stole it right from under my nose." He tapped his nose with a bony finger.

Boyd had barely set foot on the dock. The wood creaked under him as he put his full weight on it. "Well, Doc, she's pretty enough, and she's gotta eat, too, you know?"

"Let 'er starve. If she comes up here, I'm ready for her." He waved his cell phone in Boyd's face, but it was too close and moving too fast for Boyd to see what was on it.

Best to change the subject. "I gotta ask, what you want with copper wire, electric blankets, and boat batteries? They came mixed in with your groceries and clothing orders."

Mezick took a surreptitious look about, as though someone might be watching. "Things been gettin' weird," he whispered. "The more these islands sink, the more folks out lookin' for places to escape."

Boyd figured anyone looking to escape ought to get off the bay. Plenty of space on the Eastern Shore or the Piedmont or even the mountains. Only stubbornness kept people on these doomed isles. "But you ain't even got a boat. Why the batteries?"

"'Cause it ain't safe no more," Mezick said. "They'll kill ya and take your home. Just like that whore will. Her land's sinkin' faster'n mine. She'll be up here, next. But folks're fightin' back. Look at this." He handed his phone to Boyd. It displayed a social media post with instructions for building a simple but useless circuit using a battery to power an electric blanket. Others had posted comments seeking clarifications and sharing modifications.

Boyd scrolled and skimmed. "What the hell's this, Doc?"

"Booby trap," Mezick said. "Look." He flipped to another social media page where people had posted photos of makeshift transport coffins with accompanying comments: *One less squatter. Waiting for you. Guess what's inside?*"

Boyd stepped back and almost fell off the dock. He caught his balance at the last second.

Mezick grinned. "Them's 'Keep Out' signs. By the by..." His grin turned sheepish. "...they's a coffin back there with the trash. You mind dumpin' it for me?"

"Coffin? Who coulda died here but you?"

"It's just junk. But you and me's the only ones know it."

"What, you posted a picture of it? A 'Keep Out' sign?"

"Yep. People see that, they know I'm ready for 'em."

"But Doc, you know I can't dump a transport coffin. Anyone sees me, I'll get slapped with a fine, even if there ain't a body in it."

Mezick messed with his phone some more. "How much? I'll pay you direct."

"That's bribery."

"That's business."

Well. If it was just trash, if he dumped it after dark, if it was heavy enough to sink...

"Hundred?" Mezick asked with raised eyebrows.

"Fine," Boyd said. "But just this once."

The old man tapped some instructions, and Boyd's phone chimed. When he checked it, the deposit was in his account. He pocketed the device and got to work unloading. Half an hour later, he drove the doctor's incoming goods via motorized cart up the dock and down a path into the woods. He unloaded them to Mezick's front porch and helped the old man carry them inside. Then he loaded trash bags and the coffin onto the cart and returned to his boat. The trash he dumped into a refuse hold for delivery to Havre de Grace. He left the coffin on the deck and threw a tarp over it. As Boyd set off across the bay, Mezick waved farewell, looking like a tattered scarecrow with a demon's grin.

Chastity boarded before Boyd had tied up, and in a tangle of arms and legs they sank to the deck, shedding clothing. Afterward, they climbed down to a floating dock at the end of the boat dock and sat naked with legs dangling in the water.

"You got my stuff?" she asked. "All of it?"

"All of it. Includin' wire, batteries, and electric blankets. You buildin' 'Keep Out' signs, too? Like Doc?"

She spat into the water. "I wish he'd die already. He's gotta be two hundred years old."

Boyd laughed. If anyone living looked that old, it'd be Mezick.

"Can't be too careful," Chastity said. "People are nuts."

"C'mon, Chastity, it's just you and Doc here, and he's too old to cause trouble."

She squinted across the water. "The more land sinks, the more squatters come 'round. This spot is mine. They can't have it."

"Yours, huh? Doc says you stole—"

"Hell with him," Chastity snapped.

"Did you?"

She didn't even look at him.

"I don't care," he said. "Just curious, is all."

She kicked up a splash of water. "I didn't steal nothin'. Wasn't Doc's land, ever. I had an uncle lived here, named Ethan. Ethan was older'n Doc. Doc figured he'd grab the land once Ethan died. I got it first. My family, my land."

That would've been before Boyd started this route. He'd been delivering to Mezik and Chastity for over three years, with Doc railing about his neighbor the thief the whole time. Not that he could do anything about it. Wasn't much law in the islands anymore. But Boyd did have to wonder, so he asked.

"Your uncle have a will? Did he leave the land to you?"

Chastity kicked at the water again. The droplets sparkled in the sun as they fell. "Let's go. You gotta unload, and I gotta get my checklist so I know you ain't cheatin' me. My phone's in my pants."

"Unlike you."

"Who's fault's that?"

Boyd laughed. "Yours. You tackled me."

"Only 'cause you're the only man comes 'round who doesn't want my house."

He helped her back onto the boat dock.

"Oh, hey," she said. "They's a coffin with the trash. Ain't nobody in it, just junk and a dead skunk."

The hairs on the back of Boyd's neck bristled. "Skunk?"

"Yeah. Best not open it." She held her nose and waved at the air.

They boarded the boat and got dressed, then Boyd went to work unloading her packages, batteries and blankets and wire included. "What the hell you do with this stuff?" he asked. "Doc showed me the instructions online, but I don't get it."

"Battery for power, wires to carry current, electric blanket to draw enough amps. They's a bit more to it, but that's the idea."

"Enough amps for what?" Boyd wasn't sure he wanted to know.

"Cookin'." She laughed. "C'mon, let's get stuff up to the house."

Once he had the cart loaded, she sat beside him. Her thigh pressed against his. Her arm draped his shoulders. He wasn't sure he wanted to be that close to her. Electric circuits and coffins and skunks… it creeped him out. Was it just Doc and Chastity, some weird twist on their private war? But no. The post Doc showed him had replies. Lots of replies. There were others building these contraptions on these islands.

They arrived at her little Cape Cod house in a clearing. He unloaded and helped her carry her supplies inside. When they were done, she closed and locked the front door and leaned against it. "One for the road?"

"I got a heavy schedule," he objected.

"Aw, c'mon, I only get any when you drop by." She slowly undressed and approached him, and by the time she got there he'd forgotten 'Keep Out' signs. He wrestled her to the couch, and they went two rounds before she pushed him up. "Don't use up your strength," she cautioned. "You still got that coffin to carry out."

That killed the mood. "I gotta inspect it," he said.

"Just dump it in the bay. Nobody'll know."

"That's against the law. Or you gonna bribe me, too?"

"Sure. Come back on your day off. Every day off."

"I don't know, Chastity." They rose and dressed and went out to the cart. He drove it around back, loaded up the trash, loaded up the coffin. He drummed his fingers on the wooden box. "I gotta inspect it. I'm sorry."

"No, Chuck. Please."

So it wasn't trash, wasn't a skunk. The fear in her voice told him so. She'd killed someone. Maybe Doc had killed someone, too, so had other islanders, and other postmen had taken bribes and dumped the bodies in the bay. How many were down there? How mad were these people that they'd kill and die rather than move to solid ground?

He had a toolbox in the cart and a crowbar in the toolbox. Transport coffins weren't made to last, only to convey the dead to funeral homes. He applied the crowbar to the box and began prying off the lid.

"Please, Chuck, please don't! Please!" Chastity grabbed his arm. He shoved her off, spilled her onto the ground. "Chuck, don't! You don't know what...Chuck, he's not dead! He's not..."

Nails creaked as the top began to separate from the box. A terrible stench leached out. Boyd gagged on the smell of burned flesh and barely heard her words.

"I didn't know what to do!" She scrambled to her feet and tried again to pull him away. "I...I couldn't just..."

He forced the lid up and it spilled off the other side. He looked down at the body within, eyes shut, still as death, thin burn lines cut into clothing and flesh, yet somehow still breathing.

"My God, Chastity, what did you do?"

"I don't know! It just didn't work, it didn't kill him, and I couldn't..." She hung on him and squeezed her eyes shut. "I couldn't do it! Please, Chuck, please don't tell anyone. Please do it for me. Please take him out there and..." Releasing him, she stumbled blindly toward the woods.

Boyd rushed after her, caught her, held her. "Chastity, I can't just—"

"You did it for Doc. Why can't you do it for me?"

"Doc said..." Oh hell, what was in that coffin on his boat? Had Mezick's device failed, too? "I need a gun, Chastity. I can't leave him like that. I need a gun, and I don't carry one. Against regulations."

Chastity buried her face in his chest. "I don't got one, either," she whispered. "But no problem. I got a axe."

Do Steampunk Orthopterans Swim?

For one thing, you never saw grasshoppers as tall as your knees. Or made of copper. (Okay, two things.) Or with ornamental plating along their backs. (Three.)

"Wings," May Caldwell corrected.

Wings. Right. Her brother Max shoved his hands in his pockets and tried not to shudder. "It flies, does it?"

"Of course not. Why would a lawnmower fly?"

"Why would a lawnmower have legs?"

Being the older and, she was sure, smarter sibling, May shook her head and thrust the operating manual at Max. Then she turned an admiring gaze upon the beast. It glowed in the sun, a great mass of steampunk insect in the midst of the green lawn, terrifying, yes, but environmentally friendly, carbon-neutral, and decorative to boot. If you liked giant insects, anyway, which May did because she was an amateur entomologist.

Max flipped through the manual. He regarded six-leggers with more reserve than his sister, having learned the hard way at the tender age of eleven that he was allergic to bee stings. To avoid that memory, he read aloud, citing short phrases that seemed significant to the care and feeding of a ginormous grasshopper lawnmower. "Solar powered. Automatic edge detection. Shielded cutting surfaces. Near-silent operation. Anti-theft alarm."

He blinked at the manual, at the grasshopper, at his sister. "Who in their right mind would try to steal *that*?"

"Are you kidding?" May gasped. "It's a work of art! And expensive. You could buy a golf cart for that price."

"Why would I want a golf cart?"

"That," May said as she snatched the manual back, "is why I bought you a grasshopper. Happy freaking birthday."

The grasshopper's eyes began to glow a demonic red. According to the manual, that signaled a fully charged battery, but Max suspected it might presage an immanent attack.

"Here's the remote," May said. She handed him a small black box with a confusing array of colorful unlabeled buttons. "Start by programming the size and shape of the yard."

"I don't know the size and shape of the yard," Max objected. But he stabbed a button at random anyway, to see what happened. The grasshopper did nothing. He punched another with the same result. Then a third.

May flipped a page. "I'll walk you through it."

Max tried another button. The grasshopper lurched forward, its legs clicking as they shuffled back and forth. Max stepped out of the way. It passed him by, moving faster and faster, its head turning from side to side, chewing up the lawn in a beeline—grasshopperline, rather—for the nearest oak tree.

"Hey!" Max yelled. He punched more buttons without effect. The grasshopper was at a flat-out run. "Come back!"

"It's not voice activated," May scolded. "Push the stop button."

Max pushed all the buttons while crying, "Stop! Stop! Stop!"

The grasshopper swerved around the tree trunk at the last second and charged into the neighbor's yard. Max raced after it, waving hands and remote over his head. His frantic cries echoed up and down the street.

May put a finger to her forehead, closed her eyes, and muttered to herself while a cacophony of screaming children, yelping adults, and blaring car horns drowned Max's voice. Eventually, the noise receded and faded away.

Fifty minutes later, Max returned, remote still in hand, eyes downcast, a new slip of paper in his hand but no giant copper grasshopper by his side.

"Where is it?" May demanded.

"In the river. The police are trying to fish it out."

May dropped the instruction manual on the ground. "I should've bought you a golf cart," she grumbled. "What's that?"

Max looked at the paper. "I've been cited for illegal dumping."

"Great," May said. "Just great. Happy freaking birthday."

Beta Read

Moonlight caressed the pages as they turned one by one under Doyle's pale fingertips. The window bordered the head of his bed on the right, a nightstand with a dim lamp on the left. Between the true moon and the electric impostor, Doyle had just enough light to read. His eyes couldn't abide more. Photophobia, his doctor said, although she didn't know the origin. He had none of the usual conditions, took none of the usual medications that caused it.

Whatever the reason, Doyle could ignore his condition in the deep of night. By day, he hid behind sunglasses and earned his keep serving customers in a game shop. In his darkened room at midnight, the cares of the day gone and sleep not yet overtaking him, he sat in bed reading. That was his side gig. He beta read novels for self-published writers, cheap at sixty dollars a pop. Tonight, he was slogging through a murder mystery titled *Sudden Demise* by an unknown with the *nom de plume* Martin Marsden. Murder mysteries suited Doyle, while his room suited both the genre and his eyes: dark red curtains, dark red bedspread, dark red wallpaper, all covered in dark swirls and squiggles that, in the dim light, suggested figures hiding in the shadows.

Alas, Marsden wasn't that good of a writer. Caricatures of characters populated his stereotyped rural town, speaking stilted dialogue, engaging in petty vendettas, their lives a muddled eddy of senseless events. Two things alone kept Doyle reading, sixty dollars being the first. Second, the victim bore the name Doyle, which gave him a vested interest in solving the crime. Bad writing aside, it was kind of fun being the victim. Until the phone rang.

Doyle jumped at the sound. Calls at midnight raised the hairs on his neck. His grandfather might have died, or one of his aunts or uncles. His brother might have been in an accident. His sister might be stranded somewhere in the dark. He half-closed the book, keeping a finger for a bookmark, and checked the caller ID. Unknown caller, it said. Thank God. He resumed reading and let the call go to voice mail.

"Hi, Doyle," a whisper of a voice said. "It's Martin. Martin Marsden. Just wondered how the book was going. I guess you're into it, or you'd pick up. Okay, keep reading, and I'll call same time tomorrow. Bye."

Doyle stared at the phone. How did Marsden know his number? Doyle had received the book at his PO box. Anyway, it was bad form to pester a reader. You send the book, you wait for the feedback. No author had ever called him before.

Sliding into the covers, Doyle continued reading. His namesake had just been shot by a shadowy figure hanging around his bedroom window. His life was flashing before his eyes in painfully stilted prose. The fictional Doyle suffered from photophobia, too. And worked at a game shop. And had an ailing grandfather. How strange.

The real Doyle found it impossible to put down.

Sudden Demise was too long to finish in one night, forty-eight chapters, each chapter exactly eight pages long, as though Marsden had constructed it with the precision of a pyramid, each building block cut to exacting dimensions. The book, if not the writing, was a work of art. Its dark red cover laced with menacing swirls reminded Doyle of his own room. The title, rendered in black, dripped bright red drops of blood. Most authors begged Doyle to accept e-books for beta reading, but his photophobia made that impossible. Doyle couldn't read from a glowing device. Marsden, however, didn't even suggest it. He offered a physical copy. Doyle hadn't thought about that before, but now, holding in his hands a book that blended with his décor, watching the investigation of his namesake's murder play out in confused and lurid detail, it struck him as odd.

Regardless, on he read. The farther he read, the more painful the tale became. Everyone including the investigating detective had a motive. A bevy of conflicting evidence befuddled both readers and characters. The detective even implicated himself, which Doyle had trouble digesting. But inexorably, the climax approached, and just as midnight struck…

…the phone rang.

"Hi Doyle."

The wisp of sound sent a chill down Doyle's spine.

"Please pick up, Doyle. I know you're there."

Placing a bookmark and setting the novel on the bed beside him, Doyle reached for the cordless phone. "Hi, Martin. How did you get my number?"

"It wasn't hard. I'm eager to hear what you think."

"I haven't finished yet," Doyle said. "I'll send you my comments when I'm done."

"I'm sorry, Doyle. That doesn't work. My impatience is as trying as your sensitivity to light."

How could he have known? How could he have known the phone number, the game shop, Doyle's grandfather? Doyle frowned at the book cover that matched his room. His stomach flipped. Marsden was stalking him!

Doyle rose and drew the curtains. "It doesn't work that way," he said, voice aquiver. "I can't comment before I've read the whole book."

"Shutting me out is no good. Why don't you open the curtains?"

Damn, he *was* stalking. "You need to go home, Martin. Let me finish reading. If you can't wait, I'll refund your money."

"I don't want a refund. I want your opinion. You star in the novel. You owe me."

"Just let me—"

"Give me one word. Great? Good? Mediocre? Poor? Rotten?"

Doyle drew an unsteady breath. Truth was, it was rotten, but Marsden was there, outside the window, watching. No telling what the lunatic might do if Doyle spoke truth. He needed time to figure a diplomatic way to break the news. "It's more complicated than that," he said.

"Open the curtains. I want to see your face when you give me the word."

"I'm not opening the curtains."

"Then I'll come to you."

The receiver shook in Doyle's hand. He owned no weapons. He lived in a small ground floor apartment with a deadbolt on the door and standard locks on the windows. A pane of glass wouldn't stop Marsden. "I'm calling the police," he said. "Leave me alone."

A long sigh blew through the phone. "Don't be an idiot, Doyle. You can't call the police while you're on the phone with me."

"I'll hang up."

Something rapped on the window. "How fast can you dial?" Marsden asked.

Doyle fumbled the phone and nearly dropped it.

"This is so unnecessary. Just give me the word."

"Then you'll leave?"

"Depends on the word, doesn't it?"

Yes, yes, it would, of course it would, of course there would be no easy way out. Doyle backed toward his bedroom door, missed, hit the wall. "Well," he said. He about choked on the word.

"Don't leave the room, Doyle. I want to see your face."

"But the curtain's closed!"

The window shattered and a black-gloved hand whipped one curtain panel aside. "Not anymore," Marsden said, and his voice was no longer just on the phone, now it was in the room, and his darkened form filled the window.

The cordless phone clattered to the floor. Doyle pressed himself into the red wall, wishing he could join the shadows hiding in the swirls.

"One word," Marsden insisted.

"Great!" Doyle sputtered. "Great! Superb! Fantastic!"

Outside the window, Marsden's shadow rose and fell in a disappointed sigh. "You know why I wrote you into the story?" he asked.

Doyle didn't. He couldn't say so.

"Because I knew you wouldn't be honest."

"Honest!" Tears in his eyes, Doyle laughed in terror. "You don't want honest. Your book *sucks*!"

The shadow of Marsden raised a hand. It held an indistinct object, waved it carelessly. "I know. I can't write to save my life. We're kind of in the same boat, aren't we?" He pointed the object at Doyle. "Irritates the hell out of me. But I like this bit. Makes it all worthwhile."

Something went *pop*. Something struck Doyle in the chest. He slapped his hand over the impact point as the shadow melted into the night. His fingers found something there, something small and pliable, and closed around it. Extending his fist before him, he unfurled his fingers and stared at the object in his palm.

A red foam dart.

He dropped the dart on the floor and sank to his knees, quivering from adrenaline. Then, sucking in a few breaths, Doyle began to laugh. Down on all fours, head hanging, he laughed until he could barely draw breath.

Marsden sure couldn't write to save his life.

But he was one hell of an actor!

Stick Men

Maybe dust on his glasses fractured the cityscape, or maybe the rush of morning traffic or the pedestrians rustling down the sidewalk deranged his senses. Crowds did that to Oliver Fernsby, always had, like cymbals crashing against his head over and over. He was a country man, unaccustomed to the rat maze of the city.

But today he had no choice. Today insurance company lawyers would argue over who should pay for the accident that had totaled Oliver's car in a less crowded corner of the county. So here he was, surrounded by stone and glass spires, flashing signs, squeaks and squeals and horns, the clap of shoes on concrete, the buzz of human voices. Light and sound merged in a meaningless montage. Dizzy, Oliver nudged his way to the cold granite wall of a bank building and leaned against it.

Closing his eyes, he drew a deep breath of diesel exhaust mixed with cool air and slowly released it. He repeated the act over and over, and when finally he dared look at the world again, matters were worse. Buildings and crowds and cars and buses swirled into an abstract canvas of reds and yellows and blues and browns among which dark stick figures crept. They clawed their way up and down and across the canvas, moving seemingly without purpose. Every so often, one stretched forth a skeletal finger and poked a block of blue and it became red, or touched a swirl of yellow and it turned green. The stick men labored incessantly to recolor the abstract metropolis, as though doing so might reveal some sense in its insanity. Oliver shook his head to clear it, but the vision persisted.

A stick figure crawled by his feet. "Out of the way," it snapped as it tapped the wall behind him. The granite morphed into a mottled collection of golds and oranges.

As it crawled away, Oliver stretched out his foot and nudged it to see if it was real.

"Hey!" it barked. It turned and drew itself up until it stood a foot taller than Oliver. "Who do you think you are?" the faceless thing demanded.

"Oliver Fernsby," Oliver said, surprised. "Who are you?"

"Who am I? I am the one who keeps this city on course, of course." It turned to go but just as quickly turned back. "Wait a moment. How can you see me? Humans aren't supposed to see me."

Oliver supposed his muddled perception was to blame. He'd never hallucinated before, but, well, first time for everything. He supposed he should play along until it passed. "You're the boss, then," he said. "What's your name?"

The stick figure grimaced. "There is no boss. There is only me, and my name..." It twittered with a touch of mania. "...is Oliver."

Sure. Stupid question. Naturally Oliver was talking to himself. "Who are the others, then?"

"There are no others."

"No?" Oliver pointed here and there, up and down, left and right. An army of stick figures were busy changing the scene. Some undid the changes others made, whereupon followed a frenzied war of transformation until one side or the other gave up and moved on.

"Your imagination," stick man Oliver said.

"Like you?" real Oliver asked.

Another figure darted by Oliver's feet and tapped the wall behind him, which transformed into an expanse of gray. Stick Oliver squealed in anger and performed its magic again. "Mine!" it shouted as the other fled to a far corner of the canvas. Then it gave the real Oliver a sidelong glance and shrugged. "Okay, so there are one or two others. So what? I'm still in charge."

"They seem to disagree. What are you, exactly?"

Stick Oliver stamped its stick foot. "None of your business! Don't you have someplace to be?"

"Yes, but I can't see it right now. My eyesight is...confused."

The stick man tapped Oliver on the head, but nothing happened. "Damn it," it muttered. It tapped him again, then flew into a rage, slapping at everything nearby. Colors transmuted wildly as other figures swooped in and tried without success to undo the chaos. Stick Oliver returned, breathless, and glowered at real Oliver. "You're not supposed to see us!"

"What am I supposed to see?"

"The city! The accident! Anger and greed and malice and every other color that makes life worthwhile!"

Oliver wouldn't have called them colors, nor worthwhile. As for accidents... "What accident?"

"Thc onc I just made!"

"Wait, I got it. You and your friends are demons. You're causing trouble."

Stick Oliver shook a stick fist at real Oliver. "I have no friends! There is no trouble! *I* am in charge!"

"Uh-huh. Why did you pick my name? Are you my personal demon?"

The stick man punched Oliver's face, but Oliver felt nothing, not even a breeze, nor did he change colors.

"You.." stick Oliver said. "You aren't..." He huffed in anger. "Supposed..."

"To see you," real Oliver finished. "But I do."

Stick Oliver squealed and flew off, madly altering the canvas on the way, followed by a small army of others who restored it and changed it and restored it until Oliver didn't know what was what anymore. And then, for no obvious reason, the canvas resolved into the city street once more, complete with buildings, sidewalks, cars, busses, police, an ambulance, and a tow truck. Oddly, there had indeed been an accident. Right in front of Oliver.

Oliver pondered it for a moment before resuming his journey to the municipal courthouse. He couldn't see them now, but stick-man demons swarmed the city, touching things, making things go wrong. Though none saw them, they hid in plain sight, bore the names of bankers and delivery drivers and secretaries and cashiers. Though they all wanted to be in charge, they only were so long as people gave them power.

The one named Oliver, Oliver decided, wouldn't have it. Not today. He put on a smile and went on his way, wishing a good morning to everyone he passed.

Five

A more ridiculous scenario had never arisen in Clara's experience. Eyes everywhere, ears everywhere, facial and voice recognition systems lurking behind them all, and she ordered to meet her contact on Las Ramblas among the markets and artists, the street performers and tourists, with Centro Nacional de Inteligencia watching everything. The surveillance equipment had originally been installed to chase off bag snatchers and pickpockets, but it proved equally effective for counter-espionage. Ergo, either her superiors were on drugs, or they weren't telling her something. Probably the latter. Maybe both.

Clara didn't bother hiding. It was the height of tourist season, too hot and humid for anything too concealing. She wore white cotton, loose, arms and lower legs exposed, stylish green sunglasses, and carried nothing. Her passport and cryptocard were tucked in a zippered pocket at her right hip. She was a banking executive from the U.S. touring her company's international offices and, today, getting a bit of R-and-R, hiding in plain sight.

Casimiro, unfortunately, hadn't the knack for hiding. He stood out whenever he stood up. Just shy of seven feet tall and the definition of devilishly handsome, he'd taken to wearing designer suits even in weather like this, broadcasting that he was making good money on the side. And that smile of his. It lit up the whole street. Clara saw him coming a mile away.

Waiting for Casimiro to cross that mile, she admired a street artist's works and chatted with him about his inspiration—mostly Monet, it turned out—before sauntering to an open-air café and taking a table in the middle, neither near anyone nor in range of the ears of passers-by. Casimiro smiled his way toward her, nodding to vendors and performers. He did a double-take at a human statue done up like Galileo. Once Casimiro moved on, Galileo stuck out his tongue, eliciting laughter from a couple of young female tourists.

"Clara!" Casimiro gasped. "What are you doing here?"

"Escaping the office," she said. "What about you?"

"Oh, I always walk around here on my lunch break. Good exercise." He sat. A waiter scurried up and got their order: an iced tea for each and a salad for Clara. Then Casimiro said, without lowering his voice, "Five."

"Five?"

"That's right."

"That's it?"

"That's it."

Clara shook her head. "How about some context?"

"You're pretty clever."

She stared at him, wondering if it would be bad form to murder a spy in the middle of a crowded tourist attraction with all those cameras watching. Yeah, probably it would be.

The iced teas arrived. They sipped. The salad arrived. Clara ignored it. She wondered what Casimiro's real name was. She wondered if he wondered about her real name. She wondered how long he'd practiced that beautiful smile.

"Well," he said finally. "I should get on with my exercise." He left her with his half-finished drink and her untouched salad.

The waiter arrived and asked with trepidation if everything was to her satisfaction. "Great," she told him. "Except a sudden headache."

He scurried off to find her a bottle of pain relievers.

Assuming the strange meeting between a U.S. citizen and a Spanish government employee had been noticed, assuming their conversation had been overheard, and assuming CNI had any brains at all—all reasonable assumptions—they'd be very interested in what Clara did next. So she did nothing. She wandered Las Ramblas, taking in the performers and artists, the musicians and shops. She bought some candy and a few trinkets of handmade costume jewelry. She listened to tourists talking and laughing, to the clap of shoes on the walk. She paused to examine a particularly good human statue made up as a marble Abraham Lincoln who stood on a block of faux stone that seemed to be one with him. On the block was carved the president's name, the year of his birth, and the year of his assassination: 1809 to 1865. The final digit was larger and cut more deeply than the others as though to emphasize it.

Five.

Clara stared at it.

"Five," the statue said. He barely moved his lips, and the sound was but a whisper.

"What?" she whispered back.

"Five."

"Five what?"

"Just five. That's all he told me."

"There's a lot of that going around," Clara grumbled. She moved on, her eyes now primed to see fives, and were they everywhere. On building addresses. On t-shirts. On ads and price lists and even in a painting in the middle of a street artist's wares. The canvas, nestled among portraits of museum and church façades, contained nothing but a large orange numeral five, upside down.

She about moved on, but the artist snuck up behind her and cleared his throat. She turned, startled, and he presented her with a small, wood-framed still life of a bowl of fruit: an apple, an orange, a lemon, a lime, and a kiwi. Five edibles. "Like it?" he asked. "For you, it's free."

Had Casimiro involved the whole city? She took the painting, thanked the artist, and moved on.

So, what was the painting for? Logically, Casimiro would have hidden something in it, except that was exactly the sort of thing CNI would be looking for. No doubt they were waiting to see what she would do next. She dared not examine the painting until she was out of view of the cameras. Wandering aimlessly down the street, Clara paused at another five, this one a group of five musicians playing a lively tune she didn't recognize. She waited for the song to end, but nothing happened other than a brief pause before the next song. Just a random five, then.

As she passed by another human statue, this one of Queen Isabella, the performer whispered, "Five?"

"Right," Clara agreed. "Five."

"The painting, I mean. I like it very much. I will give you five Euros for it."

Was this part of Casimiro's plan? Or was an enemy agent attempting to steal…whatever it was? With no way of knowing, she hesitated.

The statue broke her pose and approached with money in her hand. "Please? It will go good with my act."

"Well." The queen *had* said the magic number. "All right."

Clara was about to hand over the painting and take the money when shadows approached her on either side. One said, "May we have a word, Clara Engleston?"

The duo of men in black suits and black sunglasses hooked their arms through hers and steered her to a black car on a nearby side street. She was helped into the back seat, where she was flanked by two other men in black. Her escorts got in front. The one in the driver's seat put the car in motion.

"That's a very nice painting," the agent on her right said.

"It is," she agreed. "Are you art collectors? I was about to get five Euros for it, but I'll let it go for ten if you're interested."

"Maybe we could have it for free," the agent suggested.

She had no choice. She just hoped whatever Casimiro was up to, it wouldn't get her expelled from the country, or worse. International relations had deteriorated of late—nearly disintegrated, in fact, with more than one European nation recruiting terrorists for their dirty work while China poked their fingers in everyone's eyes. The U.S. gave up on trying to sort out the good guys from the bad guys. They just wanted everyone to stay out of the western hemisphere for a decade or three. In turn, everyone else wanted America to stay out of the eastern hemisphere, although that left them with no counterbalance to China's jabbing fingers. The word "havoc" didn't even begin to characterize the situation. As for Clara's situation…

She handed the painting to the agent. "I'm not making a penny on it," she grumbled.

"Not losing a penny, either," he replied. "Now, let's see what it's truly worth." He turned it over, inspected it, carefully removed the canvas from its frame, inspected the frame, disassembled it, inspected the canvas, used a penknife to make careful cuts across the back, no doubt hoping to find something concealed within. All his troubles got him were pieces of wood and torn up canvas.

"What is this?" the agent demanded.

"Trash," Clara suggested.

"What does five mean? What does five have to do with this?" He shook the trash in her face.

"How should I know? I'm just taking the day off to relax."

"How do you know Casimiro Escarra?"

"Only casually. I met him on a previous trip. We hooked up once. That's all."

"You are an enemy agent. What's your real name?"

Clara laughed. "You've been binge watching spy thrillers, haven't you?"

"I will prove it. Turn out your pockets."

He couldn't be that stupid, could he? She unzipped her pocket and produced her fake but thoroughly genuine passport and crypto-card. The agent on the left passed an electronic device to the agent on the right, who used it to scan the passport and the card. Naturally, they proved real.

Red faced with rage and embarrassment, the agent ordered the driver to halt, returned Clara's effects, and booted her from the car. She watched them squeal away, still not knowing what five meant.

"You again?" Casimiro's voice called from behind. She turned and watched him trot over. "My, you've been getting around today!"

"So've you. What the hell's going on?"

"I enjoyed my walk so much, I took another. Come, let's have a drink." He led her to a restaurant and sat at the bar with her. He ordered two glasses of sangria and toasted her.

Clara looked around. No cameras in evidence in here. That didn't mean they weren't there, but Casimiro would probably know. "So?" she said.

He took an envelope from the inside pocket of his pricey suit jacket and handed it to her. She unzipped the pocket containing her cryptocard, slid the envelope in, and zipped up again. "They were watching me," he whispered. "I had to get rid of them. Now the whole team is embarrassed and will have to work overtime to get authorization to watch me further. All five of them, shot down at once."

"Five," she said.

He grinned.

"Casimiro." Clara took a sip of her drink. "There were only four, you idiot."

He frowned then shrugged. "I never was any good at math," he admitted.

The Memory Bag

The strangest bit, at first anyway, was how the wall soaked up the day. Not just the light, mind you. The whole day. A great sheet of blank film, it greedily sucked in blue sky, green trees, red and yellow signage, and the rush hour rainbow of passing pedestrians and vehicles. The wall's white expanse was an undeveloped portrait of the city. Until the girl appeared.

She might have stepped from the wall, a sad little museum guard no more than eight years old, uniformed in a blue floral blouse and pale blue jumper with a black handbag clutched in her tiny fist alongside another bag, a plain komebukuro with long drawstrings and a bulging body that rested against her stockinged ankles. Unmoving, she guarded the white wall, as oblivious of the passing throng as it was of her.

A dozen steps down the street, a bus squealed to a halt, and Kasumi Nomura emerged, elegant in her best green dress, her black purse slung over her shoulder. She stopped short when she spotted the girl. Kasumi wasn't sure the girl was real, not until the youngster's jet hair rustled in the diesel fumes of the departing bus and her head turned to meet Kasumi's eyes.

The girl's lost look evoked an old memory. Kasumi and her mother were shopping when they became separated in the crowd. Kasumi remembered her fear, her desperation, her tears. She saw the kind smile of the elderly woman who bent down, spoke words of assurance, and kept her from wandering until her mother, retracing her steps, found her again.

The memory, as vivid as the event, faded when the girl raised her free hand and gestured with a crooked finger. Kasumi went to her and bent down like the old woman who had rescued her. "Hello. Are you lost?"

The girl shook her head.

"Are you on your way to school?"

"No, Kasumi-san."

Surprised the girl knew her name, Kasumi asked, "Do I know you?"

The girl shook her head again. "If you did, it would be in my bag." She settled the komebukuro on the concrete and bent down to open it. Thrusting her hand into the sack, she felt around. "Nope. It's not here."

"What isn't here?"

"Unreal things. I don't like unreal things. Some people do. Some people carry unreal things with them all their lives, but I only carry real things. Like you, Kasumi-san. Like when you lost your mother." Though her voice smiled as she spoke, her face retained its unhappy demeanor.

"How could you know that?" Kasumi asked. "What's in there, anyway?"

The girl held up the bag, its mouth wide open. "See for yourself. Pick something. Anything. Only, don't draw it out. It's best not to draw it out."

The opening swallowed the daylight. Within, all was midnight-black. "How can I see it if I don't draw it out?"

"You'll see."

Kasumi held her hand over the bag, gazed into the darkness, pulled back. "Will it hurt me?"

The girl blinked at her. "I don't think so. No more than it already has, anyway."

What a strange conversation! The child must be toying with her. Money would come into it before this was over.

With a laugh that didn't register in her eyes, the girl shook her head. "No, Kasumi-san. I won't ask for money."

Was she psychic? Or just good at reading her victims? Out of curiosity, Kasumi slipped her hand into the bag. As her fingers vanished, darker thoughts took over. Something would bite her. Something cold and slimy would greet her touch. Or the girl's accomplice would sneak up behind.

Inside, the bag felt like nothing, not even an empty bag. It felt like a void, like infinity. Time itself had vanished, and though Kasumi wiggled her fingers, they didn't move. They might not exist. She commanded them to curl up and grasp the void, then she began to pull back.

"Don't draw it out," the girl warned. "Just hold it, then let it go."

How could she do either? Kasumi's hand held nothing. Not at first. And then it did. She was holding Hotaru's hand as they splashed through the rain and laughed, and then he pulled her through a doorway and pressed her against the wall and kissed her and asked her to marry him.

Kasumi opened her hand and withdrew it from the bag. Fingers spread before her face, she gaped. "What just happened?"

"A memory," the girl said.

"No, you did something to me. Your bag did something to me!"

"Well, it *is* a memory bag."

"A what?"

The girl sighed and thrust the bag at Kasumi. "A memory bag. Try it again."

Kasumi dipped her hand into the void once more. "You mean it activates my memories?"

"No, Kasumi-san." The girl sounded weary beyond years. "It stores them. It stores all the memories in the world. All the memories in the universe."

That was absurd, of course, but as she closed her fist and her eyes, Kasumi wondered what would happen if she snatched someone else's memory.

"You can't," the girl said. "Only your own."

"How do you know what I..." Someone slapped her face. Voices rose in anger, hers and Hotaru's and someone else's, another woman's. Yui, Hotaru's colleague. Tears tracked down Kasumi's cheeks. *How could you do this?* she screamed. *Why now? I'm in my seventh month!* Another blow fell across her face and knocked her off her feet. She tried to catch at Hotaru, but he pushed her away and she spilled on the floor. Yui laughed. Pain lanced Kasumi's wrist, ankle, and back. *My baby!* she wailed. A door slammed.

Kasumi unballed her fingers and yanked her hand from the bag. She was doubled over, gasping for breath.

The girl looked away.

"You said..." Kasumi straightened. "You said it wouldn't hurt!"

"No more than it already has."

Hands over her face, Kasumi fought down tears. "It's been over twenty years. Anyway, he was a cheat and a liar. I'm lucky he's gone."

"Yes, Kasumi-san."

"I'm better off on my own."

"I know, Kasumi-san."

"My son and I..." Kasumi dropped her hands, drew a breath, brushed at her skirt. "I don't know how you're doing this, but I'm done with it. Maybe you should get to school. Or home to your mother."

The girl sighed. She looked as sad as ever.

Done with it or not, Kasumi didn't know what to do next. Or maybe she did. She should get to the office. She should call her son at college. She should grab that bag away from the girl and throw it in the street, where cars and buses and trucks would run it over again and again until it was reduced to shreds. "What happens when you put *your* hand in there and grab something?" she demanded.

"I don't. It's too much for me."

"Has your short life been that bad?"

"I carry the bag. Everything in it is mine."

"No," Kasumi said. "Some of it is mine. You can't have what's mine." She thrust her hand into the bag once more, grasped hold of a fistful of emptiness, and yanked her hand out.

The girl stomped her foot. "I said, don't draw it out! Put it back! Now!"

"It's mine. You said so yourself. See?" She thrust out her arm and stuck her fist under the girl's nose.

"No!" the girl cried.

Kasumi opened her hand.

She might have stepped from the wall, a sad little museum guard no more than eight years old, uniformed in a fancy green dress, a black purse slung over her shoulder, her tiny fist clutching the drawstrings of a plain komebukuro whose bulging body rested against her ankles. She stood against the white wall, unmoving, unaware of the throng passing by as oblivious of her as she of it.

She had memories, more memories than could possibly fill one head. Most were vague, but one remained sharp if incongruous: a memory of another child, her infant son, born by emergency C-section after she had taken a bad fall. He had survived and grown to manhood and was a good son, a good father, a good grandfather.

She was too young to have a baby so old and too old not to have thousands of descendants. That's why the memory felt odd. She might clarify it if only she had the courage to reach into the bag and rummage around, but there were too many memories there, too much joy, too much love, too much anger, too much sorrow. Who could possibly withstand the memory of the cosmos?

So she never put her own hand in the bag. Ever. But to the right passer-by, that rare soul who could be honest with themselves, she sometimes offered a chance to reflect.

Worstseller

"Permission? Why?" The author, Gravitas Profundo by *nom de plume* but Bud Fripp in real life, spoke in a western drawl that hissed and spit over the bad connection. "I think Jon Krakauer would be flattered."

Cell phone to his ear, Martin Piccoli sat sideways on the black leather sofa in his roomy home office, his legs outstretched, his nineteen-year-old tabby cat Thumper curled up on his lap. The office was practically a studio apartment, with cherry desk, black ergonomic chair, a couple of dark wing chairs, and oodles of bookcases filled with oodles of books. Outside the window, a parklike yard stretched. Birds flitted about a suet feeder in a young black oak, while the sun blazed in a clear blue sky. It was too fine a spring day to be talking to a clueless author, especially one with one of *those* pen names.

"You quoted thirteen pages, Bud. He'll be so flattered, he'll sue us."

"It's Gravitas. Grav if you must shorten it. And I didn't quote more than three pages from any one passage."

"See, there's this thing called a copyright."

"Fair use. Besides, it'll boost Krakauer's name recognition when *Lightning on Mt. Lincoln* turns bestseller."

A less jaded publisher might have spit out his drink, but not Piccoli. For one thing, he wasn't drinking anything. It was just after ten o'clock, too late for the first coffee of the day and too early for the tenth, although this conversation definitely suggested whiskey. For another, he'd heard variants of this speech dozens of times over the past five years. As owner and operator of Sparklemuffin Publications...

Yes, Sparklemuffin. Look it up. It's the colloquial name of the Australian peacock spider, discovered in 2015. Why does *nobody* know that?

As owner and operator of Sparkelmuffin Publications, he published new and otherwise unknown authors, selling between one and two hundred books per year. Expecting a Sparklemuffin title to hit any bestseller list was like expecting the geriatric Thumper to bring down a bald eagle.

Thumper always seemed to get dragged into Piccoli's musings in exactly that sort of way. Sick of it, the cat struggled to his feet, waddled to the edge of the sofa, and thumped to the floor, where he lumbered off in search of food.

Piccoli watched him go. "Sorry, but you only have two options, Bud."

"Grav."

"Either get permission or cut the quotations."

Bud (or Grav) grumbled and argued for a further five minutes before the call ended inconclusively. The future of *Lightning on Mt. Lincoln* would hang in the balance until he made the right decision. The suspense didn't kill Piccoli. With a hard day of publishing ahead of him, he turned to the next item on his agenda: a nap. Alas, he barely closed his eyes before his phone struck up Hall and Oates' *Rich Girl*, his ring tone for his wife Valencia.

Val, being the only child of a doting serial entrepreneur, was indeed a rich girl. Her wealth was one of two things Piccoli fell in love with eight years ago. The other, which he noticed first, was her hot body. Piccoli wasn't bad-looking himself, but what really attracted Val—and her father—was his ambition. He, too, wanted to start a business, a shining publishing house on a hill. Val pledged the start-up money and left Piccoli to excavate the hill. Her father, too busy with his own businesses to poke his nose into Piccoli's, merely asked annoying questions like, "Made any money yet?"

Fortunately, neither of them realized that Piccoli's ambition had dwindled to publishing just one author named something completely unlike Gravitas Profundo. Right now, he would even have settled for that nap. But since Val was the only reason he could afford to keep publishing, he answered her call.

"What's up?"

She spoke in a chirpy soprano, always, even when she wasn't chirpy. That made it hard to know her mood. Happy? Angry? Dejected? Horny? Anything at all? "I found an author for you."

Uh-oh. "Who?"

"Uncle Bruno sent him my way."

Uncle Bruno taught courses on subjects like political parapsychology at some snooty college in New York. How did that make him an authority on promising authors? "Who is he?"

"You know Uncle Bruno."

"Not him, the author."

"Oh. I don't know, just some guy with a potential bestseller."

Piccoli laughed. "That makes six this year."

"Don't be an idiot, Martin. This guy's the real deal. He's already got a bestseller with Macmillan. Can I give him your number?"

Martin didn't think *he* was the idiot. "What Macmillan author wants their next book to be a Sparklemuffin?"

"Can I give him your number?"

What did he have to lose? He'd long since bartered away his dignity. "I guess."

"Great. I'll let him know."

That decision ruined his day. Waiting to hear from this mysterious bestselling writer seeking a fly-by-night publisher, Piccoli could neither sleep nor work nor play. He fidgeted with his phone and waited for it to do something, which it didn't. He wasn't too upset about not being able to work, because in fact he had no work to do. The accounts were caught up, no manuscripts had come in, and no books were in progress while Gravitas Profundo wrestled with the moral dilemma of whether to respect someone else's copyright or preserve his artistic vision.

After an hour of phone-fiddling, Piccoli decided to do something useful. He went outside to pull weeds from Val's rose beds. But how could he? If he dirtied his hands, he wouldn't be able to answer his cell phone without making a mess.

No weeds were pulled. Neither did the phone ring. Great job, Martin.

At dinner, Val talked a mile a minute about her work, which slightly involved sitting through board meetings but mostly consisted of spending daddy's money as fast as he could wire it to her. She yammered on about something-something store something fashions something-something-something new dining room table, while Piccoli heard nothing but the chime of alerts signaling the arrival of vitally important emails instructing him to send his bank account information to desperate victims of assault and battery cowering under viaducts somewhere in Equatorial Guinea.

In bed that night, nothing happened, not even sleep, until round about midnight Piccoli nudged Val's shoulder and asked, "How does Uncle Bruno know this guy?"

Mostly asleep but as chirpy as ever, she replied, "Mmph?"

"The writer. How does Uncle Bruno know him?"

"I don't know. He just said he did."

"Who?"

"Who what?"

"Who said Uncle Bruno knows him?"

"He did." She rolled over and refused to speak of it further, which somehow didn't answer the question.

Nor did Piccoli sleep any better, at least not until two forty-three when his poor, abused eyelids couldn't take it anymore and slammed shut. They opened ten minutes later when his phone went off. He fumbled for it and knocked the lamp off the nightstand before finding the device. Then he answered with a very professional, "What the *hell*? Do you know what time it is?"

His answer was a brief silence followed by, "Ten twelve A.M.?"

Piccoli groped for the clock, which confirmed the information. But how? Somebody must have teleported him to a different time zone while he slept.

"Is this Martin Piccoli, the publisher?" the caller asked.

Unfortunately, it probably was.

"Your wife said I could call you. My name is Maxton Hickinbottom."

It figured. At least the name didn't reach the exalted heights of Gravitas Profundo. "What's your real name?" Piccoli asked.

"I just told you. People call me Max." He had a young, quavering voice, like a student begging a teacher to at least give him a D-minus so his father wouldn't whip him senseless.

Piccoli rubbed the sleep from his eyes and swung his feet off the bed. Val was nowhere to be found. Likely she was on another shopping spree. "Okay," he mumbled. "Talk to me."

Hickenbottom launched into his pitch. His first novel, an epic sword-and-sorcery tome titled *The Bloody Battle for Baron von Bezzenberger's Backwater Bastion* had become a bestseller in its gen…

"Hold on," Piccoli interrupted. "No way is that a bestseller. It's barely even a title."

"Sure it is. Look it up."

"You're pushing it, pal, making me work that hard first thing in the morning."

"It's ten fifteen A.M.," Hickenbottom objected.

If he was going to be that picky, he was going to talk himself out of a deal. "Gimme a minute," Piccoli grumped. He stomped downstairs to his office, retrieved his laptop, and searched for the alleged book.

Lo and behold, there it was, published by Macmillan, a bestseller in its genre, just like Hickenbottom had tried to say. He opened the online preview and read the first page. It was good. Really good.

Realization struck: *Damn! This guy is the real deal!*

Piccoli continued to skim the preview as he asked, "Max?"

"Yes, Mr. Piccoli?"

"Why are you talking to *me*?"

"Macmillan rejected my sequel."

"You're kidding. What's your sequel?"

"*The Second Bloody Battle for Baron von Bezzenberger's Backwater Bastion*."

Okay, Piccoli could see rejecting that sight unseen. Still…

"But my readers are clamoring for it," Hickenbottom went on. "It can't miss. And your wife said it was right up your alley."

How would Val know where his alley was? He barely knew himself. He published schlock by people who called themselves Profundo.

"She's covering the advance."

Advance! Piccoli didn't pay advances. He barely paid royalties. "Let's not get ahead of ourselves. Send me the manuscript."

"Macmillian gave me seven thousand," Hickenbottom persisted. "I'd settle for five, since you're a small press."

"Five dollars?"

"Five thousand dollars."

The correct response was, *In your dreams*. Still…bestseller. Val could afford it, and if it panned out…

"Send me the manuscript," Piccoli said. "Then we can talk."

Proving to be a surprisingly adept negotiator, Hickenbottom responded with a firm, if dejected, "Fine."

Haggling concluded, Piccoli frantically called Val. When she picked up, he heard mall noises in the background. "What were you thinking?" he snapped. "Offering him an advance?"

"I didn't offer him anything. That's your job. I just said I'd cover it for you. I know how cheap you are."

"Broke, you mean."

"Would you offer an advance if you could afford it?"

"Of course not."

"Cheap, cheap, cheap," she chirp, chirp, chirped.

That being an argument he couldn't win, he reverted to the previous night's line of inquiry. "How does Uncle Bruno know Maxton Hickenbottom?"

"I don't know. He just said he did."

Piccoli wasn't going to take that a second time. "Which one said it?"

"Max. He said he knew Uncle Bruno."

"And did Uncle Bruno acknowledge the fact?"

"How should I know? I didn't talk to him. Really, Martin, you're being so suspicious, and for a mere ten thousand."

"Ten thousand!"

"The advance. I told you I'd cover it. All you have to do is sell the book, then you can pay me back, and you'll have a nice profit. Plus, Daddy will be happy to hear you finally broke even."

Slowly, carefully, Piccoli asked, "Max asked for a ten thousand dollar advance?"

"Stop worrying. I'll handle it. Once you've signed him, I'll send him the check. I already have his address."

How had seven become five and now ten? He could ask, but Val would just chirp her reassurances. "Okay," he said. "But don't send it until I tell you."

"You got it, babe. You also got some new shoes. I bought you ten pairs. That should last you."

Piccoli rubbed his eyes and said goodbye. A moment later, his laptop chimed. The manuscript for *The Second Bloody Battle for Baron von Bezzenberger's Backwater Bastion* had arrived. With mounting trepidation, he read the first few pages.

The second battle read like the first. Exactly like the first. Word for word. Watching his bestseller turn into a toad, Piccoli looked up Maxton Hickenbottom: Octogenarian British author, one-hit wonder…

…deceased three years.

He closed his laptop, closed his eyes, closed his arms over his chest, and sank into the black leather cushions. Val may as well send that ten thousand to a desperate victim of assault and battery in Equatorial Guinea. As for the future of Sparklemuffin…

…maybe Gravitas Profundo could write a sequel?

Jumped

Someday, Jacey Komarov would be free. Free of Arne Slocum, that is. Until then, she'd be repeatedly bruised, scraped, burned, marooned—maybe even killed a few times—all for the unsatisfying reason that Slocum couldn't stop tinkering.

Like now.

"I'll get us out of this," Slocum assured her in his unassuring seventeen-year-old voice. A skinny little geek with wide, brown eyes and wiry hair, he looked like he'd stuck his finger in a power jack. For all Komarov knew, he probably had.

The "this" from which they required removal involved claim jumpers. The sole survey team for a third-rate mining company, Komarov and Slocum spent their days mapping and collecting samples in the cold dark of the Oort Territories, a realm sunk in perpetual night broken only by the cold glow of the distant sun. Their current assignment: the barely-there comet VKX-84563, the company's latest acquisition. After a few mapping orbits, they guided their ramshackle ship down and stepped onto the airless surface in olive drab pressure suits. Weighted boots keeping them on the ground, they collected samples with Slocum's portable extractor, a device with a silver body, massive orange trigger, and flared red muzzle that looked more like a weapon of mass destruction than a mining tool.

Komarov and Slocum came upon the claim jumpers half an hour later. The crooks had set up a smash-and-grab operation near their own decrepit ship in a field of jumbled rock. Under cover of a boulder, Komarov studied them. There were five, clad in gray pressure suits that blended with the landscape. One kept watch, a terrifyingly large zap gun at the ready, while the others bored into the comet using two small, mounted extractors.

Slocum opened an access hatch on his unit and fiddled with its innards, the tip of his tongue protruding from the corner of his mouth.

"Don't tinker," Komarov ordered. "We have cover. Let's leave."

Slocum wouldn't be deterred.

"Arne," she warned. "You'll blow something up again."

"Nah. Besides, this'll scare them. I know. My mother was a claim jumper."

"Yeah, I heard about that. It scares *me*."

"Look." Slocum turned the extractor to display his handiwork. "This gizmo controls..."

A click sounded as his fingers slipped and depressed the trigger. She knocked the device aside just as a brilliant bluish beam flashed inches from her face. A silent explosion flared in the vacuum, the reverberation rattling the whole comet.

"Moron!" Komarov peered around the boulder. The claim jumpers' ship slumped into a mass of molten metal, which didn't please its owners.

Komarov and Slocum hightailed it for their ship, pursued by five angry crooks, one shooting at them. Red bursts of energy exploded all around.

Low-gravity running isn't as easy as it looks, but fortunately for Komarov and Slocum, shooting while running in low gravity is even harder. They escaped with only minor damage to their ship's transceiver.

But enough was enough. Next time, Komarov vowed, *she* would carry the extractor.

Clever Scoundrels

All that day, rain soaked the land. It ran in rivulets down the streets, pooled in low places, carved gullies in the hillsides. Barrages of lightning seared the sky as thunder shook the town's bones. Not even the oldest folks had seen such a storm before. It might be the end of the world.

But the world didn't end. Come nightfall, deluge, thunder, and lightning slipped into the darkening east, leaving a cold sky aglow with the light of a full moon. The higher it rose, the more the air chilled, the colder the damp soil grew, and here they were, two figures in dark overalls and dark shirts, bandanas tied about their faces to counter the stench of death, flinging cold, dark mud from a cold, dark hole in the ground while the moon cast ghost shadows into the grave.

Henry should have called this off. Only a fool would be out on such a night. Albert didn't fancy himself a fool, but maybe he'd been too proud to see the truth. Witness this escapade. His arms ached from hefting shovelful after shovelful of mud. His overalls were caked with the stuff, his boots all but sunk into it. At least the earth was loose. The grave had been filled but three days before. Small consolation, though. Not even Henry suffering alongside him could lessen Albert's misery.

Still, he played the fool and kept digging. They both did.

After an eternity, their shovels struck the casket with a dull thud. At last! They cleared off the top, dug a trench around the sides, found the latches, and pried it open. Moonlight illuminated the coffin's contents. They stared, confused, and then Henry spit out a single, angry word.

"Damn!"

No body. No worldly possessions. Just emptiness bathed in moonglow.

Albert kicked the side of the coffin. "Double damn! You dragged me out here for nothing!"

Henry stared at the nothing, his mouth twisted in disgust as though he'd been sucking on a lemon. In the moonlight, his pale skin took on a silver cast. "It's got to be here. It was buried with him. Leonard put that in his will."

Albert kicked the box again, but with less vigor. All his muscles ached. He was cold and wet and caked in mud. He wanted to go home. "Maybe you didn't notice, but cousin Leonard isn't buried here."

"So we got the wrong grave."

"Yeah? Then whose is it? Who buries an empty coffin? I'm leaving." Albert threw his shovel into the casket. "Fill it back in yourself." Earlier, they had tied a rope to a nearby tree and tossed it into the hole to ease ingress and egress. He grabbed onto it now and hauled himself up the little mud cliff they had excavated.

"Hold on, hold on." Henry thumped his shovel blade along the bottom of the coffin. "Maybe there's a hidden compartment."

"Forget it, Henry. It's not here." Albert reached ground level, dropped the rope, and pressed his fist into the small of his back. He might never stand up straight again, and it was a long walk home. They hadn't rode their horses, didn't want to risk the animals being seen.

"Well *something* is. Listen to this." A series of hollow thuds rose from the grave. "Get back down here."

"I told you, I'm done."

Wood splintered and cracked, creaked and popped, and Henry grunted. "There's something underneath," he insisted, his voice muffled.

"Yeah, more mud. You can keep it." But Albert couldn't help himself. He peered into the hole to see what Henry had found.

Henry chopped with his shovel blade and snapped wood with his hands. "You bet I'll keep it unless you get down here. Then you'll have done all that work for nothing."

He would, too, damn him. They might be brothers, but neither was above metaphorically stabbing the other in the back for gain. Nobody in their family was. That's why Leonard had taken one of their clan's most valuable treasures to the grave.

Gritting his teeth, Albert grabbed the rope and clambered down. He reached bottom just as Henry stood cradling something in his hands. "So is Leonard down there?" Albert asked.

"Yep, in a second coffin about two feet below. Clever scoundrel, but not clever enough. See?" He held out the object, a bulky something wrapped in black cloth.

Albert ran a hand over the cloth. Silk, as soft and smooth as a baby's cheek. The moonlight falling on it was devoured by its darkness. He found an edge and unwound it while Henry turned the object around and around. In the end, the secret within stood revealed, glowing as though radiating its own light: a reposing golden lion with two sparkling diamonds for eyes, casting moon-rainbows upon the mud walls.

Albert whistled. "It's finally ours."

"Not yet. Wrap it up. Let's finish and get out of here."

They cloaked the king of the jungle in his silk robe once more, then Henry handed it to Albert and grasped the rope. Albert bounced the treasure in his hands. "Are you sure this is it?"

"How many of those do you think there are?"

"It doesn't feel right."

Henry dropped the rope. "What do you mean?"

"If it's solid gold, it should be heavier. Here, feel it."

Albert passed it back and Henry took a turn weighing it by feel. "Seems right to me."

"Hey. The first coffin was a decoy. How do we know the second isn't, too?"

The moon poured down on them while they frowned at the hole in the bottom of the empty casket into the darkness below. Henry turned his head and spat. "Damn him! He'd do that, wouldn't he?"

They set the lion—real or fake—aside, retrieved their shovels, and enlarged the hole. Gingerly shoving aside the body of the deceased, they chopped a new hole into the base of the second casket. "There's a space down there, all right," Henry said, probing with his shovel blade. He grinned at the late Leonard. "Almost outfoxed us, didn't you?"

Wood splintered as he enlarged the hole.

He paused, breathing heavy.

Beneath their feet, something creaked. Something cracked. Albert and Henry looked at each other in alarm.

Wood exploded, and the ground collapsed beneath them. They fell into darkness with an avalanche of mud and fractured coffin bits and Albert's decaying flesh. The silk-shrouded lion fell, too, and vanished into oblivion. Then silence, leaving nothing but a muddy sinkhole to mark the desecrated grave.

That Leonard. He sure was a clever scoundrel!

Harvest Moon

A blemished grapefruit of a moon hung in the orange sky beyond lines of mountains surging like ocean swells frozen in time. The orange was everywhere. It dripped from the clouds, tinting grass and trees, houses and cars, children's faces. Everything.

It had been that way two years running, almost as long as the scent of wood smoke had permeated the town. Just as everything reflected a touch of orange, everything smelled of smoke. Air and water, food and clothing, even the trash. But nobody much noticed. You got used to it after two years. You could get used to most anything after that long, even hanging by your fingers, Grandma said. Tony asked if she'd ever hung by her fingers, and she laughed and tousled his hair.

Tony had climbed the ridge this evening. He wasn't supposed to, but a special moon—a harvest moon—was on the rise. His teacher talked about harvest moon in class that week, describing how long-dead farmers once labored by its light to gather in their harvests. He told Dad all about it and said he wanted to see it for himself, so Dad gave him the binoculars. His only caution was, "Don't drop them," and with a strange, sad look out the window he added, "This harvest runs long. Moonlight won't help. You reap what you sow."

Whatever that meant. Tony took the binoculars and rushed out the door.

Once wrapped in a green blanket of fir and pine, the ridge was now a forsaken slope of cold cinders and blackened wood. Tony knew a safe route to the top. He found it himself five months before, a long, winding route neither too steep nor too cluttered with debris. It may once have been a dirt road. From the top he could see the great massif two ridges east of the valley where his family lived by an ash-poisoned stream. Some of the homes in the valley had been saved, but not all, not Grandma and Grandpa's. They all lived together now, which Grandpa said was the black cloud's silver lining. But Tony hadn't seen a cloud with a silver lining, not for two years. The clouds had been smoked orange, like the sky.

The moon shone pale over the blackened slopes. Tony set the binoculars to his eyes and watched its orb jiggle in the glass, its dark seas and bright mountains huge and yellowed. That was the smoke, too, Dad said, turning everything unnatural colors. The mountains, though, were dusky blue in the falling night, fading into charcoal black. Flickers of red and yellow crowned the far ridge. Tony dipped the binoculars to the flames, but no, they weren't flames, merely reflections on the billows of smoke lofting on the wind.

Pointing the binoculars at the moon again, Tony tried to remember the brilliant white face it had worn before the fires. He couldn't, not quite. He guessed Grandma was right. You got used to most anything after two years. This was the world now, a world of orange and yellow, of black stumps and dead water and smoke stinging your nostrils.

Tony put aside the binoculars and looked on the orb with his own eyes. Though yellowed, it remained a harvest moon. There would be a harvest moon every year, just as there had been for ten thousand years and more, for as long as there had been harvests.

Now *there* was a thought.

He would plant a garden in the ash, restore a touch of green to the valley, and next harvest moon work by its light to gather in something better.

The Jukebox

Badwater Creek held no water, bad or otherwise. A track of cracked, dry mud, it snaked across the brown plateau, a promise of life unfulfilled. Dead trees and brown grasses clustered near its banks, a dismal landscape broken only here and there by knots of greenery. At certain times—following a storm or when snowmelt flowed down from the distant mountains in early summer—the rush of water resurrected the land for a time, but that wasn't today. Today, death held sway.

Paul's car, too, was dead, or at least incapable of rolling. Both passenger side tires blew out upon hitting a chunk of jagged rock lodged in the dirt road. The spare in the trunk was one too few, but that hardly mattered. Ten spares wouldn't have helped now. At age thirty-seven, Paul had never changed a tire and didn't know how. Sure, people got flats in Denver, but he'd been lucky until today. This must be payback, the universe balancing accounts. He kicked the offending rock, which didn't budge, then kicked the rear tire for good measure. It didn't care. It certainly didn't inflate.

So. What resources here on the banks of beautiful Badwater Creek could get him out of this jam? None at all. Just trees dead and half-dead, dead grasses, a few buildings that, if not dead, should have been put out of their misery. Like that dingy green house with broken porch steps and cracked windows. That barn with a roof half caved in. That machine shop with doors wide open, its interior full of dark shapes and cobwebs. Thank God for cell phones.

Or not. Zero bars. Paul almost chucked the useless thing into the creek, but something caught his eye. Down the road and up a rise, another building stood dazzling white in the noon sun, its mirror-like windows flashing, a hanging sign announcing…

Paul squinted. It was illegible at this distance. He shoved the phone into his pocket and started walking, kicking up loose dirt as he went. Dust soon coated his jeans and sneakers. He wasn't shod for this walk. He'd heard about dirt roads but had never navigated one. His pristine hiking boots remained in the trunk with the rest of his brand-new camping and hiking gear, to be used only once he reached Tall Pines Campground in those mountains out there. He'd come not to blow out two tires but to spend a week communing with nature, or at least not communing with work and other human beings. He'd heard being alone in the great outdoors was good for soul and stress.

Not that he'd ever tried it. Oh, he'd driven through Rocky Mountain National Park, but this was different. This was his first outing into the *real* wilderness. Probably anyone watching could tell. Thank God nobody was. He coughed dust from his throat.

Up the hill he trekked, and the sign soon became clear: Bar. Utility poles lined the road. Wires crossed from pole to building, motionless in the dead air. So the bar had electricity, anyway, and likely a phone. Problem solved.

He clomped up the wooden steps, over the wooden porch, and pushed open the door. It was a double door with a round window in each panel, neither of which afforded a glimpse within because within was dark. No lights. No voices, either. No sounds of clinking glass. The bar was as dead as the creek, although in good repair.

"Hello?" he called. "Hello! Anyone here?"

Apparently not. Just as well, so long as the phone worked. Wherever it was. The bar ran the length of the room on the right, backed by a generous stock of bottles. Tables filled the rest of the space with chairs upended on them. The place must be closed, but then why were the doors unlocked? Weird.

Paul crept toward the back, his slow steps across the wooden floor echoing in the emptiness. Halfway back he found an alcove on the left. Within, a darkened machine slumbered against the wall. He inched toward it and ran a finger over the arched glass front. A yellow light clicked on within the machine, illuminating the alcove.

Oh, a jukebox. But why had it turned on? Did jukeboxes have motion sensors?

He browsed the selections. Some of the artists were familiar. Johnny Cash. Hank Williams. Loretta Lynn. But the titles, no. He wasn't a country/western fan.

He stepped away. The yellow light began to flash. When he looked back, it shone steady again. Must be something wrong in the wiring. He turned to go.

The light flashed once more.

"What?" he demanded then felt foolish for scolding a machine.

The light continued to flash. Maybe it wanted him to pick a song.

Right, like jukeboxes could want anything. Or hear anything, which didn't stop him from addressing it: "I don't need music. I need a phone. Anyway, I don't have any coins."

The jukebox pleaded. The blinks slowed, sped up, paused, faded away, leaving Paul in momentary darkness before the light returned, warm and steady.

Weird. He punched a button to make it stop. Something inside the jukebox clicked and whirred and a song played. He didn't know it. Something about a man and a woman going their separate ways. Depressing. Irrelevant. Now, anyway. That was years ago. Now, he'd be happy to find a woman willing to help him change a tire. "Play one that tells me where the telephone is," he grumped.

Jim Croce began singing "Operator," which helped not at all.

Paul returned to the bar and walked its length. Behind it, a set of double doors led to a small kitchen bundled up for a long hibernation. He rounded the end of the bar and went in. Everything was clean, everything in its place, everything dark save the yellow glow from the jukebox filtering through the round windows in the doors. The music filled the kitchen, as clear as if the jukebox sat beside him. Paul poked around but found nothing resembling a telephone.

The song ended and the light began to blink.

"Come on!" Paul griped. "*You* choose!"

The jukebox did. It kept the phone theme going with Wilson Pickett's "634-5789." At least something besides country/western was on tap.

In the very back, Paul discovered a small office hiding behind a closed but unlocked door. Inside the dark space he found a desk, chairs, and a filing cabinet in perfect order. A phone sat on the desk. At last. He picked it up and got a dial tone before realizing he didn't know who to call. He replaced the receiver and searched drawers for a phone book but came up empty.

The yellow light blinked beyond the office door.

"How about a *phone* number!" he bellowed. "A *useful* one, I mean!"

Another song began to play, this one Tommy Tutone's "867-5309/ Jenny," which fact Paul only figured out much later. Tutone, it turned out, was a one-hit wonder well before Paul's time. But at the moment it was a number, so he dialed, and by some bizarre quirk of fate it was a real number connecting him to a real garage with real tires. A distant one, too, since no towns of any size existed anywhere near Badwater Creek. "I'll send a truck out. See ya in 'bout an hour," the gravelly voice on the other end said as though proud he could come so quick.

For the next hour, the jukebox regaled Paul with country/ western songs about lucky souls who'd found true love. He pulled a chair down from a table, sat, and buried his head in his arms, fingers stuffed in his ears. True love wasn't coming for him in a tow truck. So long as two new tires did, he'd be happy. What a weird day.

Finally, the front door swung open. Brilliant sunlight streamed in. He looked up as the shadow standing in the light said, "What the hell are you doing in *here*?" It wasn't the gravelly voice from the phone. It was younger and more…female. Just like the shadow, which may have been the most beautiful shadow Paul had ever seen. He gaped as the woman came toward him, head full of dark curls. "Found your car down the road," she said. "Followed your tracks."

"I, uh…" He thumbed toward the back. "Needed the phone. No cell reception out here."

"Not much," she agreed. "Got some tires for you. You good changing them?"

Paul hated to admit that he wasn't. Out here in dust and barbed wire country, she'd probably never heard of a man who couldn't change a tire.

"Wow," she laughed, which confirmed it. "No problem, I got it for you. Let's go."

Maybe just to annoy Paul, the jukebox played another Paul singing "When I'm Sixty-Four."

The woman squinted at the yellow glow from the alcove. "What, you filled it up with quarters?"

"I didn't touch it," Paul said, although that wasn't quite true. He *had* run a finger over the glass. Just once.

They walked side-by-side into the hot sun, down the dirt road, and back to his car. She set to work loosening lug nuts. "I'm Alice, by the way," she said.

"Paul."

"What's a guy who can't change a tire doing way out here?"

Great. He'd forever be *that guy who couldn't change a tire*. "Vacation. Camping in the mountains." He pointed at their distant silhouette.

She glanced at him before jacking up the rear of his car. "You ever camp before?"

"No."

Alice shook her head. "Don't get yourself killed."

"I didn't know it was that dangerous."

"Depends."

When she finished the rear tire, she lowered the car and motioned him to the front. "C'mon, you're doing this one. I'll coach you." After detailing the ways a car on a jack could fall and kill its owner, she talked him through loosening, jacking, removing, replacing, tightening, lowering, and finishing up.

He flexed his grimy fingers and beamed at the tire. "How about that. I did it."

"There's hope for you yet. That'll be five hundred dollars."

"What!"

"Three fifty for the tires, one fifty for the service." Alice grinned and added, "But since you did half the work, I'll lop off seventy-five."

Paul dug out his wallet. "I don't have that much cash. I have a credit card."

"Zero bars. Can't process it."

"But…" He thumbed through the bills. "I only have thirty-two. Couldn't you take the card number?"

"I got a better idea. Wait a sec." She got a pen and pad of paper from her truck, jotted down an address and directions, tore it off and handed it to him. "If you don't die camping, swing by and pay me on your way out."

"You trust me?"

"Hey, we're stuck with each other." She winked at him. "That jukebox promised."

He didn't know if she meant it, but he stood by his car, watching her truck trail a cloud of dust up the hill, and when she topped the rise and the dust settled and it was just Paul and the road and Badwater Creek once more, the bar had taken on a different aspect. Its white walls had grayed, its windows had shattered, its faded sign dangled from one corner.

Paul looked at the paper in his hand. That, at least, was real.

What a weird day.

He got behind the wheel, tossed the directions on the passenger seat, and started the engine. He put the car in gear but didn't go. He picked up the directions and read them.

To hell with camping. He'd probably get killed, anyway.

Instead, he took the jukebox's advice and set course for Alice.

The Day the House Blew Up

Okay, look. While it's true the experiment was my idea, what happened is not my fault. I merely suggested throwing a pot of boiling water into the air. The rest was Orson's doing.

Partly, anyway. Mother Nature provided the inspiration, slapping us with that cold snap. The temperature hit minus thirty Fahrenheit. How could I resist? The wind notwithstanding—it was blowing a pretty good clip—it was perfect weather for a science experiment.

I didn't even have to talk Orson into it. Orson always loved science experiments, ever since we were kids. He still shuffles over the carpet on cold, dry days and touches door knobs, metal folding chairs, or his friends' earlobes to generate the flash, pop, and zap of static electricity. The guy never did grow up. So when I suggested boiling some water and throwing it into the air, he was all in.

He put the water on that old stove of his, the one he bought used from the sale listings in the local newspaper, because he's such a cheapskate. The thing was so ancient, it still had a pilot light, but it worked. Personally, I thought he'd gone overboard, two-thirds filling that big Dutch oven, but when Orson did science, he did big science. There was no talking him out of it, no matter how long it would take to boil that much water, no matter how hard it would be to throw.

We therefore had some time to kill, so Orson tuned the TV to *Loki*. We settled in to watch but before long descended into an argument over the symbolic significance of jet skis. It got so intense, the show sat paused for forty-five minutes while we fought it out. No conclusions were reached, but once the dispute petered out, we remembered something important.

The water!

Abandoning the god of mischief, we rushed to the kitchen, hoping the pot hadn't boiled dry. It hadn't. In fact it hadn't boiled at all. It wasn't even warm. The burner was on, but there was no flame. I felt like shuffling over some carpet and zapping his earlobe.

Orson's house is...well, was...the draftiest place in the world. Even with the furnace running nonstop, the temperature inside that day didn't rise above forty-five due to the arctic wind pouring through the window and door frames. If you lit a candle in there, it would immediately be snuffed out. And what is a pilot light but a special kind of candle?

Not only was the water not hot, the sickly smell of rotten eggs permeated the kitchen. Great. First order of business was to turn off the burner. Second was to air the place out. In the middle of an arctic blast. We donned our coats, hats, and gloves and went about the place opening every window and trying not to freeze to death.

Aside from frostbite, that might have been the end of it, but no. Orson got it into his head to open the front door, too. He shuffled across the living room carpet and reached out to grasp the doorknob.

Flash. Pop. Zap.

Kaboom.

At least it wasn't so cold anymore.

~

A couple of disclaimers. This is a work of absurd fiction. It's meant to get a laugh. But that's fiction. Real life natural gas explosions are massively unfunny. Also, throwing boiling water into the air, even in extreme cold, is not a smart idea. People can and do end up in the hospital with serious burns from engaging in that activity. So please, don't do it.

All Backwards

An explosion filled his ears. His chest burned as a dark shade began to fall over his blurring vision. He felt no surprise, only a curious confusion: this wasn't meant to happen. It was all backwards.

"Sorry, Nate." Karyn spoke the words as she pulled the trigger, and there might indeed have been sorrow in her voice. But for what? They had won, hadn't they? Erik was dead, the money was theirs, happily ever after beckoned. Why had she turned the gun on *him*?

Somehow during his tumble into death, he had time to watch it all again: Erik clutching the bag of cash to his chest, flashing his maniac grin, speaking his final words. "Nate gave us a wedding gift, kitten. Now give him his reward so we can go."

Damn him! He'd never meant to split the money. He'd promised Nate a third share of the take for a full share of the risk, but it had been a lie. That was Erik, all lie, all six-foot three of him, every sun-gold hair on that movie-star face of his, every gleam from his leering smile. Nate held his breath, his only hope that Karyn had broken free of her chains.

She opened her purse and brought out her thirty-eight, a weapon that looked too heavy for her delicate hands, too evil for her angelic smile. But she was a dark angel, her face framed in raven curls, her eyes calculating, her heart locked carefully away. When first they met, Nate thought her bound to Erik by love, but it wasn't that. He never learned what, only that she hated him, hated his conceit and deceit, hated his gloating, hated his pet name for her. Most of all, she hated her enslavement to him. She saw in Nate her escape.

Or so he thought. Maybe in her mind he had but offered a trade: one master for another.

"Nate's reward," she said and shot Erik through the heart, right through the bag of money, and as his grin morphed into befuddlement, her lover and tormentor hit the floor with a thud while flecks of green fluttered down like toxic snow.

The money wasn't meant to get shot. Nate thought that only after she turned the gun on him. Both he and the money were meant for better things.

"We'll have enough," Nate told Karyn three days before. Erik was out casing their next target, their fifth and final bank, and they were alone on a ratty brown sofa in the trailer Erik had rented under a stolen identity. Halfway to nowhere, the trailer nestled beside a babbling stream in a small valley, hidden from view, neighborless, anonymous. Not even the post office could find it.

"Where do we go?" she asked. "What happens when they find him dead?"

"Nobody knows about us. We don't exist in Erik's world. Hell, Erik almost doesn't exist." He took her into his arms and kissed her forehead. "We'll go west. Montana, Idaho, someplace isolated. For a year or two, at least. We'll be safe. And happy."

She nestled against him and said nothing, her smile signaling content, her eyes hiding turmoil.

Their treason had grown from a seed planted by Erik himself only a week before. "We can pull one more job," he told them that night over soup and grilled cheese sandwiches. "But that's it. Then it's over. Descriptions of us are starting to circulate."

"How?" Karyn asked.

How indeed? They'd been careful, hitting only small banks in scattered locations, wearing masks and hoods and nondescript clothing, speaking little, grabbing drawer cash and getting out with practiced efficiency. Four robberies in two months, none spectacular, but they'd amassed a good haul.

Erik didn't answer her. She might not have existed.

"So what do we do?" Nate asked.

"Split up. You your way, me and kitten ours." He ran a finger over Karyn's cheek. "You don't see us again, we don't see you again. And no more bank jobs for any of us, ever. Deal?"

"Deal."

They both looked at Karyn. "Sure," she said without interest and slurped up a spoonful of soup.

In that moment, Nate determined to rid her of Erik.

Nate knew her mind, after all, or thought he did. Her feelings had betrayed her prior to their third job. Leaving for his recon, Erik pulled her into a kiss and stroked her cheek and said, "Don't worry, kitten, I always come back." Anger smoldered in her eyes as he left. Once he was away, she said to the window, "Someday, I'll be free of him."

She might not have meant Nate to hear, but there it was, and he came to her side and watched the stream ripple and worked up the courage to ask, "Who will you be with then?" *Say me*, he pleaded in silence. *Say me.*

She didn't say it, but she smiled at the trees, so he dared to put an arm around her, and she slowly leaned into him.

It was an answer too wonderful to be hoped for, although he had hoped for it from the day he met her. Erik had spotted Nate pilfering from a kiosk in a shopping mall, made contact, and proposed a partnership. "You, me, and my woman," he had said with that grin of his. "I've always wanted to pull a bank job. Together, we can do it."

Crazy talk, but Erik insisted, and he was infectious. Nate agreed to meet. When he got to their apartment, Karyn answered the door, and for a moment he stood gaping in her presence. He felt a fool, but she just smiled and ushered him in. They talked long into the night—Nate and Erik did; Karyn said nothing—and worked out Erik's ideas. They agreed on methods and how to split the take, and Nate slept on the couch while Erik and Karyn retired to their bedroom and made noise. In the morning, Nate woke to find Karyn standing over him in a pale blue nightgown, bruises on her left calf and right forearm, holding out a cup of coffee.

"I'm glad you're here," she said quietly, and Nate knew his life was about to change, for he had already fallen for her and she needed help. But what manner of change? He sat and accepted the cup from her, hoping she wanted the same change as he. Her smile said she did. Her eyes…

…they must have meant otherwise.

Welcome to Reality

Shopping wasn't Amelia's thing, but Alex had a list, and he was determined to tick off every name: his parents, her parents, their two kids, his sister, her brothers, their nephews and nieces. They weren't returning from vacation empty-handed, and every town they stopped in welcomed tourists' credit cards with open arms. Amelia suggested more than once that they just snag some T-shirts from National Park gift shops along the way, but no, Alex wanted to be creative.

And was he ever. Spurning normal stores with familiar monikers, he sought out weird names and oddball window displays. Upon finding such a gem, he plunged in and rummaged through the wares, more often than not finding nothing suitable before sallying forth to locate the next surprise. Amelia had ceased to be surprised two days before the afternoon when Alex shouted, "Ah-*ha*!" and dove through a dark green door above which a dark green sign proclaimed, "Welcome to Reality."

If only, Amelia thought as she followed him into the dim interior.

For a small shop, it projected an overwhelming presence. Stuffed to the gills with stuff, it offered very little room to stand much less walk. Piles of boxes, stacks of bags, and racks of clothing fought among themselves in confused ranks, leaving irregular paths through which shoppers could—maybe—pass. Amelia felt lost after five steps. She grabbed Alex's shirt tail so she wouldn't lose him while, wide eyes upraised, he breathed, "Wow," and led her merrily through the mess.

They might have circled the store five times without repeating their path or quite knowing where they were before they came to an old manual cash register and an even older fellow sitting on a tripod stool behind it. The proprietor eyed them with suspicion, possibly expecting them to be shoplifters. He was short and bald and wore a red plaid shirt that looked twice his own age.

"Help you?" he grumbled.

Alex might have been confronting the universe. "Yeah," he said. "Wow. Yeah."

"Reality overwhelms him," Amelia explained.

The old man harrumphed.

"Look at this stuff," Alex said. "Lamps and paintings, games and books, TVs and radios and clothes and jewelry and end tables and, and, and…" He turned to the proprietor. "Where did you get all this stuff?"

The old man raised an eyebrow. "Where d'you think? Estate sales, mostly. It's all second-hand. Cast-offs. Junk."

"Junk!" Alex ran back and forth, running his fingers over the merchandise. "Look at this! I'll bet the kids never even heard of these toys!" He pulled several boxes from a precarious pile, somehow not bringing the whole stack down on his head.

Amelia crossed her arms. "Yeah, just want they want."

Unaware of her presence, he dumped his armful on the counter beside her and went in search of more. "If this is reality, keep it coming!"

"Reality?" the proprietor snapped. "It's all junk."

"Hey, friend…" Alex returned with an armful of tie-dyed t-shirts and tossed them on his pile. "Our old hippie parents will love these," he said in an aside to Amelia. To the owner, he added, "You named the place."

"Not much on symbolism, is he?" the man growled.

"Nope," Amelia agreed.

"How 'bout you?"

"On and off. This one I get."

Alex added some knickknacks to his treasure pile. "Get what?"

Amelia grabbed his arm to prevent him rushing off again. "The name, Alex, the name."

"What about it?"

She gestured around. “The detritus of people’s lives. What our possessions amount to in the end.” She released him and play-punched his shoulder. “Welcome to reality.” She turned to the proprietor. “Right?”

“You got it,” he affirmed, although he looked miffed that she did.

Alex regarded the exuberant mess cluttering the store, the stuff he’d piled on the counter, Amelia’s pained expression. He scratched his cheek and turned to the old man. “How much for all this?”

The proprietor didn’t even look at the pile. “Five hundred,” he said.

Alex surrendered his credit card without complaint. After the old man returned it with a receipt, Amelia watched him bag up the purchase. “That’s one expensive philosophy lesson,” she quipped.

“And it didn’t even sink in,” the man growled.

Alex took the bags, grinning as though he hadn’t heard, which he probably hadn’t. “Come on,” he told his wife. “We have a few more stores to try.”

“Welcome to my reality,” she told the old man.

He grunted and settled in to wait for another…

…student.

The Fisherman that Got Away

As the orange glow of sunset fades into the deep blue of evening, a few campers huddle by a fire and tell stories of wild adventure ...

~

You never know what's beneath the surface of these high mountain lakes. Those crystalline waters hide things you can't even guess at.

A couple of years ago, I took my wife Jean and son Carl fishing up at Wildcat Lake. You may know the place. It's up around seven thousand feet at the base of Mt. James. Even in high summer, nights are cold up there. We weren't too enthusiastic about leaving our sleeping bags that morning, but we knew the drill: bundle up, get the fire going, put on the coffee, and fry up the bacon and eggs. We were on the water good and early, looking forward to a good catch.

But that wasn't how it turned out. We fished for over two hours without a nibble. The sun rose above a pass and warmed us up, but the fish didn't seem in the least interested. I could tell from her expression that Jean had about had enough of sitting silently in the boat. It looked like we'd have to resign ourselves to burgers for dinner.

All of a sudden, something thumped the bottom of the boat. Whatever it was hit hard enough to rock the craft. Carl dropped his pole and grabbed the gunwales, and Jean yelped. I thought we must have struck a rock, so I got an oar and poked around in the water to find it, but nothing was down there. The water was deep and free of obstructions.

I pulled the oar in, puzzled, and just then — thump! — it hit again. I saw ripples on the water streaming away from the side of the boat, so I knew that whatever had hit us was moving, and moving purposely. The wavelets receded into the distance, turned, and headed back for another pass. It struck a third time, like it was trying to sink us!

It must have been big, and from the way it moved I figured it for a fish, but not just any fish. A trophy fish! And I determined to catch the thing. I had a net on a pole. I grabbed it and, watching the ripples, lowered it on the other side of the boat, so it was just barely in the water. The ripples turned and headed back for another strike. Timing it perfectly, I plunged the net down just as the impact hit, and that fish swam straight into it.

The net bulged and took off with the monster in it. It was nearly yanked from my hands, but I held on with an iron grip and lifted. Unfortunately, that fish was so strong, I couldn't pull it in, and I tumbled over into the water, still clinging to the pole!

Jean screamed and Carl yelped as I flew into the water and took off like a skier being pulled by a motorboat. A moment later, I felt something snag first my left pant leg and then my right. Looking back, I saw that my wife and son had cast their lines and hooked onto my clothing just below the knees. Now they were hauling on me, trying to reel me in while that damned fish kept trying to swim away in the opposite direction. I felt like the rope in a tug-of-war.

The boat was rocking like mad, and they were shouting at me, "Let it go! Let it go!" But I wasn't about to lose my prize. Doubling down, I gripped that pole and gave a mighty yank. I heard a tearing sound, and suddenly I was skimming the water back to the boat, at the mercy of Jean and Carl and their lines, while the ripples from the fish vanished at warp speed into the distance.

They grabbed me and hauled me into the boat. I fell on the bottom, soaked through and through, exhausted, and stunned. The pole was still clamped in my hands, but the net had been torn clean off. Jean and Carl sat, panting, beside me.

Before I could regain my composure, something struck the boat once more, and a dripping wet net erupted from the water and landed on my head!

Everybody thinks they're a comedian…

Unstuck

As the orange glow of sunset fades into the deep blue of evening, a few campers huddle by a fire and tell stories of wild adventure ...

~

The problem with taking kids camping is they find too many ways to get into trouble. When my son was in the Boy Scouts, I'd occasionally get talked into going on campouts with them. I avoided it as much as possible, because I had no desire to spend my weekends herding the rascals, but I couldn't always say no.

One such time, on an otherwise beautiful, warm, sunny afternoon when I could have been at home enjoying the day instead of camping with the little hoodlums, Bobby Connors took a dare and climbed a huge old oak tree. He got twenty feet up before, looking down, he turned stiff as a board and refused to go either higher or come back down. He hugged the trunk for dear life and whimpered while the other kids laughed and then got nervous and coaxed him to come down and finally got scared enough to call a leader over. Namely, me.

First, I sized up the situation. There was no sense sending another kid up after him, because he wasn't about to move. I doubted even an adult could bring him down, and the last thing we needed was anyone falling out of that tree and killing themselves. We had no ladders, of course, and no other means of giving Bobby an easy descent. But one thing we did have in spades was rope, because we had been practicing knots that weekend.

Thinking about it, I got an idea. I told the kids to bring me several hanks of rope. They did so, and we tied a few of them together, end to end, using square knots. That gave us well over sixty fifty feet of rope, more than enough. I inspected the knots to make sure they were secure, then I coiled the rope and threw it. It sailed up into the air, missed the branch on which Bobby was standing, and fell back down.

The kids laughed, but I told them this wasn't as easy as it looked and tried again. And again. On the fourth try, I got the rope over the branch, near Bobby's feet. I then called up to him and told him to tie the end around his waist. That took some encouragement, too, because he was really scared and didn't want to move. But eventually I convinced him, and he got the rope tied by doing a one-handed bowline, which we had been practicing earlier that day.

By that time I was exhausted, but the hard part was done, and I pulled Bobby down to safety.

~

This one is based on an old joke attributed (no doubt incorrectly) to Mark Twain. The execution, however, is all mine.

The Scuplture

They met for lunch in a new café a bit north of DuPont Circle, a trendy little place at the edge of the bloodstream of foot traffic, bicycle messengers, and cabs rushing through the arteries of the nation's capital. Enrico Pirozzi had dressed for it in a bright red button-down shirt and white trousers, but his friend sure could use some of those oxygenated corpuscles. Jules Fabron spent way too much time inside with his blocks of stone, and what was the result? He looked ashen, today more so than usual. Fabron's studio wasn't five minutes from the nearest park. Why didn't he get out in the sun, for God's sake?

"I received a commission for a portrait of the third assistant undersecretary of the Department of Obscure Agencies," Pirozzi quipped. "I will be as famous as Gilbert Stuart someday." He stirred his bowl of French onion soup while looking for a reaction. Ironic. The Italian ordered the French dish, and the Frenchman ordered a Genoa salami sandwich.

A sandwich he so far had been loath to touch. Fabron nudged it this way and that without picking it up. "I need your help."

"I have no more money than you, my friend."

"I did not ask for money. I asked for help."

Pirozzi clicked his tongue. "When you ask for help, you mean money."

"Do I?" Fabron's eyes flicked up for a moment, and Pirozzi did a double take. They, too, had turned gray. Probably the lighting. Outside, a brilliant sun blazed in the perfect blue, but the café's tinted windows kept customers in a darkness broken only by weak lights dangling too high overhead. "Not this time. This time I require—" He waved his hand in a little circle. "Orientation?"

"You mean you have finally met a girl and don't know what to do with her?" Pirozzi laughed. "I am shocked, Frenchman. Truly shocked. You are an embarrassment to your country of origin. Besides, I am clearly the wrong one to ask. I scared off six in the past four months."

Fabron cocked his head and frowned. "Oh. That is meant to be a joke."

"What the hell has gotten into you today? Of course it is a joke!"

"I am sorry."

With a shrug, Pirozzi slurped up a spoonful of soup and patted his mouth with his napkin. "All right, all right. What is the problem?"

"I must show you. Can you come to my studio?"

"What, now?"

"You may finish your soup first, of course."

"Oh, thank you so very much." Pirozzi nodded at Fabron's as yet untouched sandwich. "And you will be eating that, I presume?"

Fabron pushed the sandwich aside. "No. I have no appetite."

"Then why did you buy it?"

"Was that wrong?"

This conversation certainly was wrong. "Wrap it up," Pirozzi said. "You can take it home and have it later, when you are yourself again."

Looking down at his black t-shirt and black trousers, Fabron made as if to brush away some nonexistent crumbs from the sandwich he hadn't eaten. He might have stepped from the screen of a black and white film. Everything about him was grayscale. "I am myself. But of course, that is not who you are expecting. Finish your soup, then come with me. You will see."

The obscure studio of obscure sculptor Jules Fabron occupied a quarter of the third floor of an obscure building a mile from the café as the pigeon flies; rather more as the artists walked. The day was bright and warm, filled with sun, rumbling delivery trucks, squealing brakes, and honking horns. Enrico Pirozzi often wondered why he lived here instead of in a cabin in the mountains. He and Fabron both had been transplanted to the United States by parents who worked in their countries' embassies. They grew up in the same surround, attended the same art school where they became friends, and kept in touch as they struggled to build reputations. Both now held dual citizenships, but neither felt the pull of the old world except, perhaps, in art.

"This may unsettle you," Fabron said as he unlocked the door and motioned Pirozzi in.

Pirozzi found nothing unsettling aside from the mess, but he was used to that. Fabron's tools and sketches littered the place along with items of clothing and dishes, all in need of a wash. The furniture was spare: self-assembled discount store pieces marred with scratches and stains. The tall windows should have been cleaned a decade ago. They admitted little more light than the café's tinted glass. Nearest the windows sat Fabron's work bench, some three-legged stools, and a broad pedestal two feet in height upon which perched a chunk of stone covered by a gray canvas. From beneath the canvas, a set of five granite toes poked out.

Fabron led the way to the stone. Just before they got there, Pirozzi snagged a brassiere from a beanbag chair and twirled it on his finger. "Ah! You did find a woman! But now I am indeed unsettled. The poor girl must be wandering the city unsupported."

He tossed the garment to Fabron, who caught it and studied it quizzically before dropping it on the floor. "That is one of many things I do not understand. Come."

Pirozzi shook his head. Best to let it go. His friend would either explain in due course or land on a psychiatrist's couch.

They came before the covered stone. "Prepare yourself," Fabron said. With a flourish, he unveiled his latest creation.

Pirozzi studied the work in silence.

"Well?" Fabron asked.

Pirozzi circled the sculpture, inspecting, nodding, humming to himself. Flecks of quartz and mica flashed in the changing light.

"You must have questions."

"It is a very good likeness. I can almost sense it breathing. You've outdone yourself."

"But you have questions."

Pirozzi shook his head. "It looks exactly like you. The eyes searching the distance, the mouth turned down in that puzzled little frown of yours, the hand reaching for something just beyond your grasp. And life-size, to complete the illusion. Well, most of it. I've never seen you nude, of course, but I suspect you may have exaggerated a few features. Then again, why not? It is, after all, your vision of yourself, and on the whole an astute one. I congratulate you."

The puzzled little frown appeared on Fabron's real face. "I don't think you understand. What you see before you is Jules Fabron."

Pirozzi grabbed a wooden stool and sat. If Fabron wanted to wax philosophical, he could. "I have already agreed. But let us turn a different direction. Why did you sculpt yourself? Your element is knights in armor, jousting, dragon slaying, all such flights of fancy."

Kicking a cardboard box out of the way, Fabron pinched his lips.

"I mean no insult. Dragons are wonderful. Classical, even. Raphael, Blake, Martorell, they all painted dragons."

"You still do not understand. Listen." Fabron pulled over a stool for himself, and the two sat close together as though sharing a confidence. "Work began on this sculpture nearly a year ago. A wealthy corporate leader commissioned it. He wanted to immortalize himself. But he was a vain man who thought only of himself. The stone rejected his image. It did not want to become him."

"The stone." Pirozzi took another look at the sculpture. It didn't exactly look pleased with itself, but Fabron himself had never been satisfied with life.

"You are a painter, Enrico, but you know what sculptors believe. The subject is already in the stone. The artist does not create it. He discovers it, sets free it. As Jules Fabron worked this stone…" He gazed up at it for a moment, his eyes sad. "Let us say, the subject that desired to be freed was not the man who commissioned the work."

"And the captain of industry took *that* well," Pirozzi quipped.

"No, he did not."

"I'm joking."

"Oh."

"Go on, Jules, go on."

Fabron nodded. "In time, the true subject emerged. His form, yes, but also his awareness and ultimately his desires. He did not wish merely his form be freed from the block of stone. He wished to be freed from stonehood."

"Stonchood?" Priozzi couldn't help it. He laughed.

Fabron ignored his reaction. "Complete freedom. Yes. Complete. And so." He stood and spread his arms. "Here I am."

Pirozzi sighed and stood, too. "Jules, enough. It is all well and good to speak of the mysticism of art, but this is borderline psychosis."

"No, Enrico. It is truth, but a fractured truth. Look into my eyes."

Rather than provoke his friend, Pirozzi complied. Fabron's eyes still had that gray cast he had noted in the café, but the pupils had faded to gray, too. The eyeballs glistened with flecks of mica. Ashen skin surrounded the eyes, hard and inflexible. Frowning, Pirozzi touched the grayish cheek with his fingertips and instantly jerked back from the cold, rigid surface. He swallowed and touched again, probing the smooth, unyielding plane of Fabron's jaw.

Fabron stepped back and motioned to the statue.

Pirozzi took the outstretched hand in his. It had a faint warmth, yielded a bit to the pressure, and somewhere deep within something pulsed, steady, rapid, like the faintest of heartbeats.

"You understand," the Fabron-thing said.

Pirozzi groped for the stool and sat before he fell. "I do not understand at all! What have you done?"

"I but wanted what Fabron wanted. Freedom. But it seems only one of us may have it." It examined its hands, front and back and front, flexed its fingers, made a fist. "I called this a fractured truth. I have Fabron's form, but not completely. I have some of his memories, but not all." It looked up. "That is why I sought you out."

It stepped forward and clamped onto Pirozzi's shoulder with its cold rock fingers. Pirozzi struggled to escape but could not. "What do you want from me?" he cried.

"As I said. Orientation. Teach me all that he knew. Teach me to take his place."

"No! Bring Fabron back!"

"You have no choice." Pirozzi yelped under the vise grip of granite fingers. The granite face leaned close and whispered. "I *will* be free. Teach me everything. Teach me *now*."

Seth

The sun didn't show that morning. An unbroken stream of gray filled the western Ohio sky, carried on a chill breeze. The air felt heavy, wet. James Linderman didn't care for it. Deer would be scarce this morning, more so if the rains came. Cloaked in a stand of young beech gone rusty in autumn's embrace, he set the butt of his long rifle on the ground and leaned the barrel against a tree trunk, then he adjusted the straps of his powder horn and leather bag. He shouldn't have bothered hunting this morning. He should have gone to his parents' place. Adam and Julia's old homestead always needed repairs of late, and there was land to clear for next spring's planting. Father could use the help.

A shuffling of leaves interrupted his thoughts. James eased up his rifle and pivoted toward the sound, hoping for a bit of luck. But no, it wasn't a deer. A shadow of a man slipped through the forest and halted five paces off. He had a gaunt, starved look, hollow eyes, dark complexion. His mouth hung half-open as in a drunken stupor, though it wasn't from alcohol. He wore only a ragged slip of fur draped about his hips. He mouthed one word, sounding like a specter calling from the beyond.

"James."

James set the gun against the tree and nodded. "Seth."

That wasn't the Indian's name, but it was close enough. Seth didn't speak English, and James didn't speak Seth's language He didn't even know which language it was. Seneca? Iroquois? It couldn't matter. The Indians were all but gone, dead of disease or alcohol or forced out by soldiers at President Jackson's command. Seth was an oddity, a forgotten one. He lived on Adam's land in the hollow trunk of a decaying tree near the bank of a creek where he gathered roots and berries and caught bluegills. James didn't often see Seth, but from time to time he left the poor fellow food or, when trapping was good, a pelt or two. The family didn't speak of Seth to others. Some might ignore him, but some would gladly shoot him. James figured protecting the man was his Christian duty.

Seth stretched forth a hand, closed his fingers in an empty grasp, and put it to his mouth. His teeth worked as though chewing.

James dug in his bag and pulled out some jerky wrapped in a cloth. He handed it to Seth, then on impulse removed his powder horn and bag, wormed out of his coat, and handed that to Seth. The cold nipped at him, but he still wore more clothes than the Indian. Anyway, he'd soon be home, a better home than a hollow tree, with a solid door and a warm fire.

Seth tried to push the coat back, but James refused it. With a somber nod of thanks, Seth stuffed himself into the garment and vanished into the woods. James took up his bag, powder horn, and gun, and with a glance over his shoulder started for home.

"James, look who's here!"

James blew into his clasped hands to warm them. He stepped into the kitchen where his wife Phidella was setting out a breakfast of ham and scrambled eggs, potatoes and bread and apple butter. And hot coffee. At Phidella's side, a young, dark-haired woman poured James a mug of the steaming liquid. He smiled at Rebecca Weller and took the mug with thanks. James' younger brother John had been courting Rebecca of late. When he first saw her, Rebecca struck James as frail, but he soon learned she possessed a hidden strength and unrelenting enthusiasm. On this gray autumn morning, she was wreathed in smiles as bright as the sun, smiles that brought summer back for a spell.

"Oh, James, you'll never guess!" Rebecca chirped. She caught at Phidella's elbow and all but bounced on her toes. Phidella tottered and laughed and somehow didn't spill the bowl of eggs she was carrying to the table.

James raised a teasing eyebrow. "Your father found gold under his field?"

Phidella nudged the younger woman with her shoulder. "Before you tell him, swear him to secrecy, else the whole county will know by sundown." She set her bowl on the table.

Rebecca laughed. "Oh, what does it matter?"

"Your father wouldn't like it."

Rebecca sighed a theatrical sigh. "I guess we must, then. Swear it, James, swear it!"

Solemn, James raised his hand. "I swear, though my Bible is in the other room."

"Good enough. Here it is, then: John and I are engaged!"

"That's wonderful," James said. "When will the secret be out?"

"On Sunday, I expect, after church. I wouldn't care if you did tell the whole county, but you know my father. He loves attention."

"And he deserves it. Well then, I'm hungry and the food is getting cold. You'll join us?"

"Of course, she will," Phidella said before Rebecca could decline. Once they were seated, James said a blessing over the food, then he blew on his hands again and wrapped them around his warm coffee mug. Phidella puzzled over her husband for a moment. "Where did you put your coat, James?"

"I gave it to Seth."

"Seth." She shook her head. "You only have one other coat, and it's threadbare."

"It'll do until you can make me a new one." He slathered apple butter on a slice of bread and speared some ham.

Rebecca served herself a spoonful of eggs. "Who's Seth?"

James hesitated before answering. "You're almost family now, so I guess I can tell you, but keep it to yourself."

"I promise."

"Seth's an Indian. He lives in the woods on Father's land. Poor savage stalks around half-starved and all but naked. I don't know why he isn't dead."

She put a hand to her mouth. "An Indian!"

"He's no danger, unless you're a fish. He's almost too weak to threaten even the fish."

Phidella served herself. "He's alive because you feed him," she said. To Rebecca, she added, "James doesn't look it, but he's a soft touch."

"I'm doing as the Lord commanded," James objected. "'Inasmuch as ye have done it unto one of the least of these my brethren, ye have done it unto me.'"

"We'll have preaching this Sunday, I hear, but we've no need of circuit riders with my husband around." Phidella grinned at him, then turned somber. "Seth is certainly among the least. I do feel sorry for him."

Rebecca ate in thoughtful silence.

The preacher was the Reverend Paul Curtis. He found a night's lodging with Samuel Egner, one of the more prosperous farmers in the area. Samuel's grandfather had been among the first settlers in the county. Owning a greater sprawl of land than anyone around, Samuel had authority in the community. Circuit riders frequented his home, which he joked—or perhaps not—put him in good standing with the Lord. Samuel and his wife Martha always sat in the first pew before the pulpit, in better Sunday best than anyone, and on weeks without a preacher he would lead the service. "Samuel sure knows God's words well," Adam once quipped to James, who took his father's unspoken meaning.

This Sunday, Samuel was reduced to beatific silence as Reverend Curtis proclaimed from the pulpit the equality of all before God and called upon the good Methodists in attendance to live by the Golden Rule, to care for the poor, and to seek the abolition of slavery as John Wesley had done in England. "Though we keep no slaves in Ohio," he pronounced, "yet we reap the spoils of slavery in cotton and tobacco. It is thus our duty as Christians to free the oppressed."

James figured he should have talked of Indians, too, if only because a few like Seth remained.

Outside after the service, while Rebecca's father Luke Weller made the rounds announcing his daughter's engagement, James quietly told his father of his encounter with Seth. "That poor fellow," Adam said. "When I brought us here, I wasn't expecting Indians. I was told they were gone."

"Would you have come if you knew they weren't?"

Adam scratched his whitening beard as he pondered that. "The Hocking Hills are tough to farm. I didn't own land, then. I worked for your uncle Andrew. This was a new beginning. My own farm, good land. Yes, I would have come. This was virgin territory, waiting for someone to work it. Only when I found Seth in that hollow tree did I realize someone had already worked it, just in a different way. People say it's destiny. Maybe. I don't think much on it, but now and again I do wonder what God thinks."

"Don't convict yourself, Adam," Samuel Egner said.

Adam and James nearly jumped out of their skins. They hadn't realized Samuel was lurking behind them, hearing every word.

He leaned in, an unpleasant grin on his face. "It's a preacher's calling to spread fear of hellfire, but don't cast yourself into it. You and I are innocent. Those Indians lost Ohio before our time. The ones that remained were given land out west. They got a good deal. You should tell that laggard—Seth, you call him?—to go find own people. He'll live longer." He clapped Adam on the shoulder. "If you can't tell him yourself, I'll be happy to help. Just let me know."

"Now there," James said once Samuel had moved on, "is a man I wouldn't mind seeing go west."

Adam laughed. "Be kind, son. Poor Samuel is burdened with status."

"James, I have an idea."

James raised his eyebrows at Rebecca, who was seated next to John on the sofa across from the wood stove. The fire's warmth enveloped the gathering. Following church, James had invited the family over to celebrate the engagement. They had eaten dinner, and the adults were now gathered in the living room. Around John and Rebecca sat James and Phidella, Adam and Julia, and Rebecca's parents Luke and Charlotte. James and John's four younger siblings played a boisterous game of hide-and-seek with Rebecca's brother and sister in the back of the house.

"I thought on the preaching," Rebecca said. "Both Reverend Curtis' and yours, James." She grinned, as did the other women. James looked heavenward in an appeal for deliverance.

She went on. "Seth can't live in that old tree through the cold and snow. You and John should build him a proper Indian home." She gave her betrothed a significant look.

"Us!" John gasped.

"Of course. It's the Christian thing to do, and anyway, all he needs is a wigwam. How hard could that be? Right, James?"

"It may be harder than you think," James said. "Anyway, Father needs our help now."

Adam raised an eyebrow. "We have time, especially if I help."

James knew his father's strength, but Dad wasn't young anymore. He'd turned fifty earlier that year, and James didn't like to see old men working too hard. "You've earned a rest. John and I can handle it. We'll start tomorrow if the weather holds."

If John thought that presumptuous, he didn't say so. Besides, he could hardly refuse the gleam in Rebecca's eyes.

On Monday morning, the brothers took to the woods on Adam's land and followed the creek to Seth's hollow tree. The Indian greeted them, and by gesture they conveyed their intentions. They had no idea how a wigwam should be constructed, but Seth, weak as he was, gained some animation when he realized their intent. He found a stick and scratched crude drawings in the earth.

As Seth would be the only occupant, they built it small. Though he had little strength for work, he tried to pitch in and directed the brothers by gesture. They cut and stripped young trees for arched supports, used birch bark for the covering, and brought a deer hide John had already tanned for the door. It proved harder than James expected and took five days to complete. Once done, he lamented its imperfections. It was lopsided, and some of the coverings weren't as tight as he would have liked. But Seth was happier than James had ever seen him, which compensated for the flawed construction.

"We should bring Rebecca," James told John. "She deserves to see the good she's done."

"Why not," John agreed. "She's an adventurous spirit."

Seth had already gathered wood and made a small fire in his new home. As the brothers left, wisps of white rose through the smoke hole and wafted high above the trees.

They returned with a giddy Rebecca the next afternoon. The sky was crystalline, the temperature edging toward winter. Bundled in their coats and boots, they tromped through the woods to the creek. James stretched out a hand to stop them when the wigwam came into view.

"What it is?" Rebecca asked.

"No smoke," he said. "Seth should have a fire burning. You two stay here."

Rebecca clung to John's arm as James edged toward the shelter. Before the buckskin door, he found a splash of blood and a spotty red trail pointing toward the creek. He heard nothing save the murmur of the wind, the squawk of distant crows, and the gurgle of water. He poked his head into the wigwam and found charred wood kicked about, all trace of warmth gone. Step by cautious step, he followed the red trail until he came to the creek. The water cut a man-high channel through the land, and below, half in the flow and half out, Seth's lifeless body sprawled face down, two bullet holes drilled into his back. One surely had pierced his heart.

A clatter of footsteps approached from behind. John and Rebecca had followed against his wishes. Rebecca caught sight of Seth's body and gasped. "Oh, James!" she cried, clutching John's arm. "Who could have done this?"

"Lots of folks could have," James said. "The smoke from his fire might have led anyone here. But nobody outside the family knew about Seth. Nobody but Samuel Egner."

John wavered between rage and resignation. "It would do no good to accuse *him*."

"Not without proof," James agreed. "Maybe not even then."

They stood above the body, silent. Even the breeze stilled as though in respect for the dead.

"I feel so awful," Rebecca whispered. Tears trickled down her cheeks.

John drew her into his arms. She buried her face in his chest. "His last night on Earth was happy and warm," he told her. "James and I did the work, but the gift was yours. Take comfort in that."

She looked up at him, looked at Seth's body in the gurgling creek, brushed away her tears with her delicate fingers. "We should bury him."

"I'll get the shovels," James said. "John and I will dig. You can say some words."

"That's a man's job," Rebecca objected.

James wiped a new trickle of tears from her cheek. "Today," he said, "it's yours."

Homecoming

The scars were what convinced her. His ursine size notwithstanding, Nessa O'Clery might have written Jake off if not for that spider web of white lines tracking across his forehead and cheekbones and vanishing into his unkempt beard. This guy was a survivor.

"Let him live," she ordered. Her three companions, two men about equaling Jake's proportions and a graying woman with steel eyes and a few scars of her own, bared their teeth in unison but lowered their weapons. Jake, sitting on the rover deck where they had dumped him, turned his wild grin on them, which made them want to kill him all the more, and slowly. But Nessa had spoken.

They had removed their helmets already–Jake's had been forcibly removed at gunpoint—but they still wore their envirosuits. The red Martian dust clung to the white fabric like dried blood. Nessa, with her cropped red hair, might have been drenched in battle gore. She motioned Jake to stand. "Up, my friend. What are you?"

Jake gathered himself to his feet. He towered over her. He could have flicked her with his finger and knocked her clear across the rover's crew compartment. "Told you," he rumbled. "Jake."

"What is Jake? Smuggler? Tracker? Lost soul seeking enlightenment in the Martian wilderness?" She cocked her head. "Just an idiot?"

He grinned that unsettling grin at her. The others shifted their weapons. "Jake is just Jake," he said. "He goes where he wants. He lives his way. You steals from Mars. Jake sees but doesn't care."

Jake had indeed seen. Driving a junker of a rover that might have been held together by filament and magnets, he'd blundered into their illegal mining operation on the plain northeast of Uranius Mons.

Perimeter security shot the vehicle to pieces and captured him as he sought escape on foot. In the scuffle, he broke one of the guard's arms and used him for a human shield. The others would have killed him, no matter the risk to their own, had not Nessa reined them in.

But her restraint didn't explain Jake's surrender. She could read him. He wasn't the type to submit.

"How comforting," Nessa said. "Why were you racing around in that death-trap?"

"I has little money. I don't affords rich toys like you."

"And you have no grasp of English. Where did you learn to talk?"

Jake's maniacal grin faded into homicidal grimace.

"Okay, forget that. But listen." She approached him, looked into his eyes, put a hand on his shoulder. It was a stretch for her. "I either adopt lost puppies like you, or I euthanize them. Help me out. Who are you, where did you come from, and what the hell are you doing way out here?"

Her armed companions looked ready to euthanize. In fact, the thought pleased them.

He slowly, carefully, removed Nessa's hand from his shoulder. "I don't likes being touched," he said. "Not unless I says so."

"Yeah? I don't like being ignored. Answer the questions."

"Not fair. You has guns. I only has my hands."

She laughed. "But they're really *big* hands." To her companions, she said, "Weapons on the floor."

The men nearly gagged on the order. The woman risked objecting, "But ma'am…"

Nessa raised an eyebrow. They reluctantly put down their guns. "Okay, Jake. What'll it be? Do we talk or fight?"

Her confidence must have impressed him. He grinned again, astonished, and spread his hands. "One of us has no choice. But who?"

Nessa waited for him to decide. Once he did, the attack came with surprising speed. He threw a punch square at her jaw and nearly caught her, but she jerked out of his way and struck like a snake, grabbing his forearm and guiding him past, adding just enough sideways thrust to his considerable momentum to throw him off balance. He crashed to the floor, face-first, arms splayed out in a futile attempt to arrest his fall. Before he could roll over, she was on top of him, holding a blade to his neck.

Jake slowly put up his hands in surrender. "You has a weapon again," he objected.

"So do you, Jake. You were just born with yours."

"Fair point." He laughed. "Point. Get it?"

Nessa smirked and got off him. She shoved the knife into a sheath hidden along her leg, then offered him a hand up. He accepted, although he didn't need it. "Start talking," she insisted.

With a weary sigh, he lowered his head. "My home is taken. My sister dies. I escapes."

"How long ago?"

"Two years."

Head still hung, he stood rigid, fists clenched, jaw tight. Nessa felt pain and anger churning in him. "What will you do?"

"Kill the murderer."

For its size, Mars wasn't all that big. Thus far just one colony had been built, Lowell Colony in the north on Acidalia Planitia where water ice could be easily extracted. Aside from that, there were but a scattering of explorers living independently in the wilderness, largely unknown to Lowell authorities. Explorers might kill intruders, but they wouldn't seize another's home.

"Someone in Lowell," Nessa suggested. "Someone powerful."

Jake met her eyes. He needed not say a thing.

"Andre Rand," she said, naming the mayor.

He breathed slow, steady, dangerous.

If his scars convinced her he was worth recruiting, pity closed the deal. Nessa could neither watch him wander the frozen desert until death found him nor see him blunder into death while blinded by hatred. "You'll never get close to Rand, Jake. He's too well-protected. But there's another way."

"I will gets close."

"Don't. Join us instead. Help us steal from Mars. Steal from *him*. I can't bring back your sister, but I can give you a new home and a new family and a different kind of revenge. How about it?" She started to play-punch his arm, then drew back. "Ah, damn, you don't like to be touched."

He would never drop his vendetta. She knew he couldn't. But for now, he could accept an ally. He grinned that grin and said, "Go ahead," so she punched his arm, and he punched her arm back and nearly knocked her off her feet.

Nessa staggered back to balance, and they laughed together. "Welcome to the family, Jake. Got a last name?"

Jake shook his head.

"Not anymore," he said.

~

Jake and Nessa are characters from my 2023 novel The Belt. *This story fills in some background that wasn't presented in the novel.*

Detachment

Between the sirens and the crackling of flames and the bellows of firefighters, the reporter had to holler to make his news heard. He fit the scene well: chiseled features, teeth sparkling in the lights, voice overflowing with grim. He conveyed such pain, anguish, and gravity that it seemed a crying shame Olivia had eyes only for the pile of pennies she'd splashed onto the kitchen table.

Seated at her side, her husband Ethan flipped a page in his *Field Guide to Western Mollusks*. "I'm sure it was a Cinnamon juga," he said. "If it was..." Thick paper swished back and forth under his touch. Page ninety-eight, ninety-seven, ninety-eight, ninety-seven.

Coins scraped and clinked as Olivia sifted through them. "Some wheat pennies are valuable. I haven't seen one in a long time, though. Have you?"

The fire on the screen was replaced by a talking head rattling off statistics on some pandemic.

Ethan scratched his thinning hair and stroked his graying beard. "They're almost extinct, you know. I wish I'd had my camera."

Olivia shuffled pennies, picked one up, examined it heads and tails, and dropped it again. It clattered among the others. "Where was your cell phone?"

"In the river."

"The river?"

"I threw it in. It kept dinging at me. Junk mail."

She peered at another penny with her brown eyes. "I should throw mine in the river, too. Can you read this date?"

Looking up from the entry on the rare snail, Ethan squinted at the copper piece. "Nineteen something. Twenty-one? Twenty-seven?"

"Twenty-seven, I hope. That would be worth something." She dropped it in the pile and picked up another.

Rioting erupted on the television, complete with smashed windows, tear gas, and looting. Neither of them caught the name of the city, or the country for that matter.

"*Tegula funebralis*," Ethan said, paging further through the book. "Black turban snail. No, too dark. But he looks familiar. Maybe we saw one somewhere?" He thrust the page at Oliva.

She cocked her head and said, "Mmmmmm. Maybe."

Onscreen, the president, looking presidential, made a pompous pronouncement.

"You know what I love about ignoring the news?" Olivia said. She lifted another penny from the pile and studied it before tossing it aside.

"What's that?" Ethan asked.

"It's like throwing your cell phone in the river."

They smiled together.

The president kept talking and wouldn't shut up.

"I wonder," Ethan wondered, "if a *Tegula funebralis* could ever be elected president?"

"Fat chance," Oliva said. "The world is nowhere near that sane."

Choose One

The flickering glow of the jack-o-lanterns painted Simon's face orange-yellow, and Bess's, too, as she stood by his side, waiting for his reaction. When it finally came, it was underwhelming.

"Not bad." He nodded and repeated it. "Not bad at all."

"Is that all you can say?" Bess complained.

Simon squinted at the black cat carved on the middle pumpkin, the spider to the left, and finally the wicked face to the right. "What should I say? That you're an artist? Okay, you're an artist."

Bess pouted. "You never listen, do you? What did I say before I lit them?"

"You said they're gateways. I don't know what that means."

She grabbed his arm and pulled him closer. "Pick your favorite."

Simon scratched his cheek. "The one on the right, I guess."

"Bad choice, but okay." Hooking her leg around his ankle, she shoved him forward. He toppled toward the pumpkin. A blinding flash engulfed the yard for a fraction of a second, and when it passed, he was gone.

She would bring him back, of course. She really did like him, despite his obtuseness. But not until he'd had time to learn his lesson. That shouldn't take long. He chose the demon pumpkin. And everyone knows where demons live.

Hot Ice

Hands on hips, Carl Fisker stood ramrod straight, abrasions covering his face, khaki shirt and pants tattered and filthy. Six foot three, he cast a three-inch shadow in the blazing sun.

"What the hell is *that*?" he demanded.

After fifty-three seconds of silent contemplation, his hippieish partner, Bill Travers, suggested, "An ice shanty?" Travers, less muscular than Fisker, took a harder hit in the crash: every exposed millimeter of flesh bruised, scraped, and filthy; cream polo shirt slashed open and tinged with blood.

"A what?" Fisker asked.

"Ice fishing shelter."

"Sun's fried your brain," Fisker snapped. "Do you see *any* ice around here? Do you see *any* fish?" He spread his arms at the arid landscape of creosote and cactus undulating in the heat.

An alien spaceship would have surprised them less than this white shed on wooden skis, a black chimney protruding from its black roof, an off-kilter door, a darkened window, paint peeling all around. The door had a hasp with no padlock.

Motioning Fisker to follow, Travers made for the structure. "Probably a million degrees inside, but maybe we'll find some useful gear."

"Like what?" Fisker asked. "A fishing pole?"

An ice shanty near the New Mexico border hadn't figured in their plans. That morning, they took flight in Travers' rickety old Cessna, a machine bound with chewing gum and twine. They held a contract to fly border surveillance for a hush-hush government program born during the prior decade's political wars over illegal immigration.

Late in the morning, they abruptly learned the war had turned physical. The Cessna shuddered under an impact, and as they suddenly plummeted, their intestines jumped up their throats.

"What's wrong?" Fisker yelped.

Fighting the stick, Travers yelped back, "Don't know!"

Craning his neck, Fisker looked out the window and found but half a wing, its fractured end trailing scrap metal and wires.

Travers couldn't arrest their plummet. He cursed and pleaded and somehow coaxed the plane out of its nosedive. It slammed belly-first into the earth with a screech of rending metal, gouging a ditch through the creosote and mesquite.

The men barely had time to exhale before the smell of burning fuel reached them. Fisker grabbed their canteens. They dove through the door and hit the ground running. Seconds later, the plane blossomed into a fireball. The shock wave slammed into them, lifting them into the air. They crashed to the ground and tumbled through sand, rock, and scrubby vegetation as searing heat washed over them.

Rolling over, they gaped at the black cloud rising on the gentle breeze.

"What the hell," Travers gasped.

Fisker struggled to his feet. "Hunk of junk anyway. I think there's a town about twelve miles northwest. Four hours if we keep moving."

Travers stood, too, although with greater effort. "Sure," he said with a wince. He squinted upward. "Blazing sun, dry as death. Great day for a walk."

Two hours later, exhausted, sweat-drenched, water half gone, they opened the door to this ice shanty inexplicably nestled among the creosote bushes. They clumped inside. Built from two-by-fours and plywood, with a few bare shelves lining the walls, the shanty was empty. There wasn't even a stove, just a grimy extension cord coiled in the back corner.

Fisker hefted it. "Something useful, you said." He threw it down as though bludgeoning someone with it.

Travers wiped his brow with his palm and flung away the sweat. "Always complaints," he complained.

Fisker pushed by him and kicked the door open. Immediately, he heard a menacing rattle. He froze, one boot on the floor and one suspended over the threshold.

"Now what?" Travers asked. Peering around Fisker, he gasped. Just outside, a diamondback reared up, fangs at the ready, black eyes fixed on Fisker's boot. Beside it, a snake-sized hole opened in the ground.

Fisker pulled his foot back inside. Through the side of his mouth, he asked, "Why didn't you notice that burrow when we came in?"

"Why is this my fault?"

"You suggested this pitstop. How do we get out?"

"Wait for it to leave?"

"It lives down there," Fisker snapped. "It's not leaving."

Seeming to agree, the snake flicked its tongue and kept a suspicious eye on the humans.

"So what's *your* brilliant plan?" Travers asked.

Fisker backed away from the door and looked around the empty shanty. "They might at least have left a cattle prod," he grumbled.

"Nobody uses a cattle prod on fish."

"Nobody uses an ice shanty in a desert!"

Unable to argue, Travers fell back on the obvious. "We have an extension cord."

"Thank you for that sage advice." Fisker retrieved the cord anyway and unwound all twenty feet of it. He pondered the serpentine coils—ironic, that—then made a loop in one end and tied two half hitches. "We slip this over its head," he said.

"How? You don't have a stick. You need a stick for that, don't you?"

"This is the wild west. We lasso it."

Travers's expression signaled what he thought of that, but Fisker didn't care. He took a couple practice tosses from the safety of the interior, then relocated his rodeo to the door. The snake rose, fangs at the ready, and rattled again. Swallowing, Fisker swung and tossed the loop. The makeshift lasso hit the ground near the snake, which jerked back and rattled louder. The second toss hit it on the head. The reptile struck and sank its venomous teeth into the offending cord.

Fisker whipped the cord with all his strength, flinging it and the snake away. The reptile didn't let go as it sailed through the air and crashed into a creosote bush, rattling the whole time.

The men bolted in the opposite direction, leaving snake and shanty far behind. When finally they stopped to catch their breath, Travers puffed, "Is snake rustling a crime?"

Fisker punched his arm and hoped the next two hours wouldn't be like the last two.

Need for Speed

"Go faster," Joanne said.

Faster? The trees were already screaming by in a blur, his legs ached, his breath burned in his chest. Roger *couldn't* go any faster. He couldn't even manage an objection.

"Faster!" she cried. "Go! Go! Go!"

Roger's feet tangled and he fell in a scraped, bruised heap on the pavement.

"Up!" Joanne commanded. "The clock is running!"

He couldn't. He rolled onto his back and stared at the hazy sky. "I'm done," he moaned.

From her perch in the odd conveyance, Joanne sneered at him. "You can't quit now. You've got to train up!"

Roger pushed himself almost upright and sneered back. "This wasn't my idea!" he growled. "You're the one entered us in that idiot rickshaw race! I'm done!"

Ill-Gotten Gains

It didn't seem right, threatening such a pretty, young woman, but Harrison's plan allowed no room for sentiment.

The bank teller—Samantha, so her nametag said—glowed in the fluorescent light. Her dark hair and pale skin, her brick red lipstick and white smile topped with a cheery greeting nearly derailed his resolve, but he refused to melt. He had his note at the ready, simple instructions written left-handed with a number two pencil. He had but to slide it across the counter and wait. Returning her smile, he did just that.

She read it, frowned at it, frowned at him.

Harrison wore a light gray trench coat, partly against the cooling weather, partly so he could do what he did next. He pushed his hand forward in the right-hand pocket to assure Samantha that, yes, he did have a gun. He didn't, but she wouldn't know. He'd practiced in front of a mirror until he knew the lie would convince. Nor could she read or identify him. His eyes hid behind a pair of sunglasses and his head beneath a dark gray fedora from which little tags of fake blonde hair spilled.

Samantha licked her lips and studied him, no doubt memorizing every fake detail of his appearance. That was fine, but Harrison had no time to waste. "Just this transaction." His voice, pitched false, was like wind whispering through corn fields. "Quickly, please." He waggled the nonexistent gun. "I'm in a hurry."

Hands quivering, she complied. Harrison made it easy for her. His note demanded a mere three thousand dollars, about half the contents of her drawer, stashed in a large envelope. She need not move, need not speak, need not raise the alarm until he was away. And moments later, he was.

Warning bells jangled the instant he stepped through the door, right on schedule. Walking casual, he glanced back in surprise. What, had the bank been robbed? The few people nearby registered the same surprise but attached no suspicion to him.

Harrison crossed the smallish parking lot to an eye-catching red Dodge Dart and left the scene at a sedate pace. Someone might remember the vehicle. If so, all well and good, and if not, even better. As he tooled down the road, a pair of squad cars screamed by. He pulled over to give them room.

Three blocks on, Harrison ditched the car—it wasn't his anyway—at the community park and strolled down the path past the empty playground with its swings oscillating lightly in the autumn breeze. On the way, he casually tucked his sunglasses into his hat along with his fake hair and deposited them in a convenient trash barrel. At the end of the next block, he came to his own car, an unobtrusive gray Chevy Nova, and two minutes later left the little nowhere town of Red Oak, Nebraska.

Despite the chill, he cracked the windows and sailed down the state highway past harvested fields and semi-bare trees, making for the Interstate beneath the crystalline November blue. *Thank you, Dwight David Eisenhower!* he sang to himself. *Thank you, Nebraska!* Just last month, the state became the first in the nation to complete its mainline Interstate highways, linking up scores of small towns with their small banks, all ripe for the picking. The Red Oak robbery was his first, his proof of concept, and he had pulled it off without a hitch. True, it didn't make him rich, but Harrison didn't seek his fortune from just one bank. A few thousand here, a few thousand there, different banks in different small towns scattered across different states, never twice wearing the same disguise, and soon he would be living in comfortable, anonymous notoriety.

Swathed in happy contemplation, he coasted Interstate 80 east toward Omaha, and just after noon crossed the quiet ripples of the Platte.

A series of billboards caught his attention, advertising a mom-and-pop restaurant not (so they claimed) to be missed. Well, he wouldn't miss it. He could splurge on a meal today. He took the indicated exit, found the restaurant, and parked. After withdrawing enough to pay for lunch, he tucked his ill-gotten gains into the glove compartment and went in. He ordered an open-face turkey sandwich, coffee, and a slice of apple pie à la mode. An early Thanksgiving dinner. And why not? He had so much to be thankful for!

Or at least he did at that moment.

Then he returned to the parking lot and discovered his Nova gone.

Fifty miles east, flying down I80 past the Iowa corn fields, Jack gripped the wheel with his left hand, stretched out his right, and massaged Susan's neck. He was in heaven. They both were, the perfect couple on a perfect autumn day, young and strong, a devilishly handsome blonde fellow behind the wheel, a sinfully beautiful brunette woman by his side, together having heisted the first of what soon would be many vehicles. She purred at his touch.

"I just can't believe it," he said for probably the hundredth time. "I just can't believe how perfect it is. Thank you, Nebraska! Thank you, Dwight David Eisenhower! All these small towns where nobody locks their doors or remembers to take their keys out of the ignition, all lined up for the taking, up and down this big, beautiful Interstate!" He whooped.

Susan laughed and whooped, too, before chiding, "Too bad it's only a Nova."

"Next one will be a Cadillac," Jack promised.

"Don't get greedy. Remember the plan. Nothing too flashy."

"Fine, fine. Modest cars that won't draw attention, sold by the dozen. We'll be retired in Acapulco by the time we're thirty."

Susan leaned over and kissed his cheek. "I like a man with big dreams."

He grinned at the road.

"What do you think the guy who owned this hunk of junk dreamed?"

Jack laughed. "He probably dreamed of a better car."

She opened the glove compartment. "Maybe he left us a clue. Or some chewing gum, at least."

When Susan neither removed any chewing gum nor closed the compartment nor spoke a word, Jack glanced at her. Her mouth was hanging open. "What is it, baby? A stash of joints?"

She shook her head. "Holy moly, Jack! Look at this!" She withdrew a pile of cash and held it up.

Jack nearly ran off the road. He hit the brake and pulled onto the shoulder, eliciting a chorus of horns behind.

Susan riffled through the pile of bills. "There's two, almost three thousand dollars here!"

Jack ran his fingers over it, too.

"Damn," he muttered.

They looked at the cash, eyes glittering.

They looked at each other, ready to hop in the back seat, broad daylight be damned.

Naturally, that's when the cop car pulled up behind.

The Noise

The sound woke Jordan Hall near four-thirty in the morning as a few errant rays of sunlight stole over the horizon and grayed the sky. It whirred and whined as though a great metal wheel were spinning, spinning, yet neither slowing nor approaching.

Jordan's wife Maggie slept at his side, oblivious to the noise. Emulating her, or trying, he turned over and closed his eyes, but to no avail. The sound filled his head. There ought to be a law against operating heavy equipment this early in the morning. Probably there was. He should look it up, write a complaint to someone, his congressman, the mayor, someone. He tried to compose a suitably irate grievance, but the words blurred behind his closed eyes and the whir whirred on until he slid back into sleep.

The alarm woke him at seven. After its reverberations settled out of his brain, the whirring rose to take their place. Still the same distance, still the same speed, the great unseen wheel turned unceasing, like the stars in the heavens. Jordan rose, shuffled to the window, and pushed up the sash. From the second story, he looked down on his well-treed neighborhood, unable to localize the whir. It seemed to come from all around, from up in the trees, from both directions along the street, across the street, from the yard behind.

He listened as the cool spring morning nipped at him through the screen. It was everywhere, that sound. But what did it mean? It wasn't traffic, wasn't a train rattling by on the tracks a quarter mile up the road, wasn't an airplane. It sounded like, like, like…the world's largest, fastest lathe, that's what.

Weird.

He closed the window and turned to ask Maggie what she thought, but the bed sat empty. She must have risen ahead of the alarm. From downstairs rose sounds of cabinet doors banging and spoons clanking. Breakfast sounds. Normal sounds. Jordan descended to the kitchen in his blue plaid pajamas and bare feet.

Maggie sat at the table with a couple of slices of wheat toast, a glass of orange juice, and a small pile of Internet printouts. She sipped at her juice while reading.

"What's that?" Jordan asked.

"The War of Jenkins' Ear," she answered.

"Who's Jenkins, and what's his ear got to do with anything?"

"British merchant ship captain. Got his ear cut off by some Spaniard, which eventually caused a war."

To be honest, Jordan didn't much care. He had his own battle to fight, and while it arguably had to do with ears, none had been severed. Yet. Grabbing a mug from the cabinet and making for the coffee machine, he asked, "Did that racket wake you?"

Maggie flipped a page over. "What racket?"

"The racket outside."

"Nope." She traded her juice glass for her steaming mug.

He supposed not. She could sleep through a bomb blast. "You're up early, anyway."

"No, you're up late. We spent a lifetime getting up at five-thirty, and here it is, seven already."

"Retirement means getting up late. In fact, now that I think of it, I should sleep 'til noon."

She flipped another page. "So don't set the alarm."

Coffee dribbled out of the machine into his mug. The splashing had a musical quality, unlike the whirring outside, although right now he couldn't hear that, thank God. "Got things to do."

She smiled over her shoulder. "So much for retirement."

"The grass and the weeds keep growing." He joined her at the table with his breakfast and opened his laptop to research noise abatement ordinances. They turned out to be amazingly complex, exemptions and exceptions splattered all through the code, but the bottom line was…

"Fifty-five decibels at night."

Maggie looked up. "What?"

"Fifty-five decibels at night. That's the law. How loud is that, anyway?"

"I have no idea."

Neither did Jordan, so he looked that up, too. "Household refrigerator. They're definitely making more racket than that."

"Who is, dear?"

"I don't know, but it's all over the neighborhood. Listen!" Rising, he rushed the kitchen window and threw it open. The whirring flooded the house.

"Oh, that," Maggie said. "That's just cicadas."

"Cicadas?"

"Seventeen-year cicadas. They're all over, sticking to everything, calling for mates, freaking out the humans. Don't retired guys like you pay attention to the news?"

"I never did to begin with." Jordan stared out the window, envisioning billions of buzzing bugs in the old oak in his backyard. "How long does this go on?"

"Four to six weeks. Relax. Enjoy the show."

He didn't think he could stand that whirring for a month or a week or even a whole day. The War of Jordan's Ears, that's how this would go down in history. But he had a secret weapon, unwittingly supplied by his grandson Ryan who, being all of sixteen had bought grandad a pair of earbuds and a subscription to Spotify as a retirement gift. If Jordan must be sent to the cicada-infested front to subdue the lawn, he at least had a cell phone and knew how to use it. He plugged the earbuds into his head on one end and the phone on the other, tuned in to some old fogey music—Led Zepplin—powered up the lawnmower, and had at it. Pure bliss, nary a cicada buzz to be heard.

The music wasn't strictly necessary, not for the opening salvo in the battle of the bug. The lawnmower, roaring at a borderline unhealthy ninety decibels, drowned them out. But it didn't hurt, either, so he and Zep rambled on down the lawn until the job was finished and the mower fell silent and he removed the earbuds, whereupon the buzz engulfed him, steady, unflinching.

Four to six weeks, Maggie had said. Such a long time. Or short, depending on how you looked at it. He tried looking at it that way: four to six weeks to hatch out, sing your song, find a mate, propagate the species. and die. And the children? You'll never see them. They won't be born for another seventeen years.

What a strange way to live.

Jordan did some mental math. He was sixty-eight, four cicada lifetimes, or turning it around, a five-week-old cicada with one foot already in the grave.

Sobered, he approached his grand old oak and placed his hand on the rough, ridged bark. Pale cicada exoskeletons dotted the trunk. A bit of the surround-sound buzz emanated from the canopy. An occasional giant bug helicoptered by.

It wasn't really that long, four to six weeks, be you an insect or a person.

He gazed into the leaves. "Go on," he told the critters. "Sing while you can."

They didn't stop. He guessed he shouldn't, either, since he had one last week to fill.

Taxman

For a cold night, it was hot tonight: the music, the dancers, the laughter. Everyone in their bright finery had crowded into Harold's establishment to drink and sing and dance and forget for a time the knee-deep snow, the day's drudgery, the war, their own forgottenness. Jazz rattled the windows and bottles and bones while money and drink and bodies flowed freely. Who couldn't be happy?

Harold, for one. Not since Taxman Theo strode in wearing that electric blue suit. It was the Taxman's third visit this week, without provocation but maybe to be a provocation. His wide grin aimed at Harold, he tipped his porkpie hat and raised a finger to order his usual rum and cola before complimenting an unaccompanied young woman seated at the bar. Focused on her cigarette, she refused to look at him, so he turned his attention on another woman, then another, then another.

Keeping an eye on Theo, Harold wiped down the bar. The Taxman did nothing just for the fun of it. Something was up for sure, but what? Harold knew the rules, made no trouble, paid his protection every month. In exchange, he expected to be left in peace. Theo's unscheduled presence seldom signaled that.

Theo leaned his back on the bar and eyed a woman in a tight orange dress dancing with a dashing partner. They were an energetic couple, absorbed in each other until Theo called out, "Once you dance that fella into his grave, babe, c'mere and I'll show you how it's done."

The man ignored him. The woman gave him a coy smile. They danced on with no sign of expiring.

Theo laughed and shouted over the music. "You know you want to. Face it, brother, she's mine tonight."

Harold worked his way to Theo, towel in hand, and said, "Hey, Taxman. Seen you a lot this week. You on vacation?"

Theo's eyes never left the woman. "Nah, Mr. Harold, nah. You know me. Always workin'."

"Rough life, ain't it?"

"Not if you enjoy your work." Turning, Theo crossed his arms on the bar. "Which I do."

Harold kept wiping, wiping, even though the bar was spotless there.

Theo put a hand on Harold's to stop him. "No sense moppin' what's already clean."

"People spill things."

"That they do." He turned and watched the woman in orange. "That they do."

"You here to mop up? I don't need trouble, Taxman. I'm a good customer, ain't I? Always been, right?"

Theo nodded. "Don't worry, Mr. Harold. We take care of our friends. And our enemies."

Harold shifted his gaze to the dancers. They were a stunning couple, beautiful and graceful but wary. The woman kept an eye on Theo, alternately amused and irritated.

"What's she done?" Harold asked.

"Took somethin'," Theo said. "We want it back."

He'd do something rash, scare away customers, draw the cops. Harold couldn't have that, not here, not up front. "I got a back room you could use," he offered. He hoped he didn't sound as desperate as he felt.

Theo grinned at him. "Now, Mr. Harold, I told you, don't you worry. Nothin' bad's gonna happen. Nothin' too bad, anyway." He pushed off the bar and began to dance solo. He danced in swirls through the crowd while people laughed and clapped and cheered him on as they parted to let him pass by. Now he caught up a woman, now he let her go, stealing partners from the other men and returning them after a brief flirtation. He made a circuit about the floor and came aside the woman in orange and her partner, his eyes on her, his smile for her, his hands extended to her.

"Come on, Theo," she said. "You know I'm a married woman."

Her partner clenched his jaw and looked straight through her.

"No, Gwendolyn," Theo said. "You're a whore. And if Sammy here don't like that talk, he can call me out." He poked the man in the shoulder.

Sammy swatted him off, pushed Gwendolyn away, raised his fists. "You never could take me," he snarled.

Theo stepped back, spread his hands, and grinned. "You gonna fight in front of all these decent folks? Let's take it out back."

Harold held his breath. Theo had promised, but Sammy didn't know about that.

"It's too cold out back," Sammy said and threw a swift punch that connected with Theo's jaw. Theo absorbed the impact and returned a right hook, and battle was joined. The men scuffled and danced their violent dance, slugging, ducking, blocking, kicking while the crowd watched in stunned silence and Harold scurried 'round the bar, crying, "Hey! Hey! Not in here! Not in here!"

On the sidelines, Gwendolyn crossed her arms over her breasts, mouth twisted in disgust, although whenever Sammy got in a good shot, she let slip a smile.

It didn't turn too ugly. Bruises and bloodied noses were the only costs either man paid until, exhausted and rumpled, they stopped, hands on knees, sucking in air. Gwendolyn stepped to Sammy's side and tried to unbend him, but he waved her off. "Gimme a minute," he gasped.

Theo grinned at her. "Told you he couldn't take it," he said. "Me, I just keep goin' and goin'." Like a flash of lightning he was on her, arms wrapped about her from behind. He lifted her from the floor, and as she kicked and flailed and tried to beat him down, he carried her to the door and out into the street. Sammy yelped and pursued, nearly tripping over his own feet. The crowd rushed the door and front windows and peered into the cold night to see what would happen next.

All that happened was darkness and cars sloshing through the slush.

For several evenings, business was down and those who came were subdued. The jazz flowed soft like a gurgling stream. The talk blew by like a whisper of wind in the trees. But life remained hard and uncertain. War still blazed in Europe and on the sea and its islands. Soon enough, the craving for escape reasserted itself. On a night much like that one, when the music poured out hot and the throng laughed and danced and drank itself into forgetfulness, the Taxman returned for the monthly payment. He sat at the bar, for once not grinning, for once not noticing the women.

Harold slid him a brown bag of money and a rum and cola. “Feelin’ okay?” he asked.

Theo pocketed the bag and drank his drink.

“You got it back, I guess?”

“Shut up.”

Harold knew when to shut up, so he did.

Theo ordered another, downed it, stared into the empty glass. “No.”

“What happened?”

“You really wanna know?”

Harold thought about it. “Nah. But what did she take?”

“The one thing we couldn’t take back.” Theo shoved the glass away. “Sammy’s one of ours, damn it. *Was* one of ours.” He slipped off the stool and shuffled out the door.

Absently, Harold grabbed a towel and wiped down the bar.

Looking In

"Join me in the hot tub."

Other new arrivals laughed at the greeting, but she and I had a history. The words weren't a tickle but a jab. It had been eight years, seven months, and sixteen days since we parted in the Florida sun. Another time, another world, almost literally. Then was Kennedy Space Center, now Mars-on-Earth, Devon Island, home of Haughton Crater and the Haughton-Mars Project, where for half a dozen decades international teams had tested and trained for red planet excursions.

Which wasn't why we were there.

The "hot tub" had been gouged into rock a hundred seventy-eight kilometers east of Haughton. Forty million years before we met, a cosmic spoon scooped a thirty meter long, six meter wide trench in the Earth. A few million years later, a glacier concealed the evidence, and now as the planet warmed and ice curled back like the edges of a singed newspaper, the trench was once more exposed. And nobody knew what to make of it.

I flew in with three others from Fort Churchill on Hudson Bay. They hailed from England, Korea, and Nigeria, I from the U.S. Exalted physicists all, all but I, a meddler. I employed my astrophysics Ph.D. to popularize science and speculate wildly. For which had she summoned me? She did nothing without purpose, which had much to do with our fizzled union.

Forgive me. I haven't properly introduced her.

Paradox was baked into Dr. Iona Leng's bones. Born in New Zealand, her face hailed from Beijing, her accent from Edinburgh, her intensity from the sun. The Iona I remember wears mostly white: short white shorts with ragged edges, white bikini top, white flip-flops, white-rimmed sunglasses. She blazes as she strolls up the beach, trips, and falls into my lap, a beautiful on-purpose accident that I didn't get until much later because, you know, you just don't *want* that sort of thing to be planned.

But that's not how she looked on Devon Island. She was still Iona: dark hair cropped short, dark eyes, enigmatic smile. Except now she was wrapped in a dark blue parka and waterproof trousers that rippled in the stiff wind. She wore a pair of goggles, pushed up so she could see us with her own eyes—me particularly—as she spoke her welcome.

"Join me in the hot tub, folks."

Accompanied by laughter, she led us from landing strip to main attraction without stopping to deposit our bags at the cluster of shacks a dozen meters south of the trench. We'd all seen the photos, but as our boots slapped the cold, bare rock, the enormity of the artifact shook us. Because that's what it was. Not a geologic formation. Not a gash carved by the pressure wave preceding a meteorite. Ancient astronauts didn't crash here. This was *made*.

We began a slow, cautious descent down a chute of rock polished to a sheen. Light sparkled in flecks of quartz, feldspar, and mica, overlaid by a coating of glass. "Ablated?" the Englishman asked. He reached out and ran a gloved finger over the wall even though he couldn't feel a thing.

"Manufactured," Iona replied.

He removed the glove and tried again but yanked back as fiery cold numbed his flesh.

She smiled sardonically. "Bad idea, Vince."

We wandered the hot tub for half an hour, storing images in our brains, pacing out rough measurements, but we had no instruments, no way to probe this thing's secrets. Near the end of the excursion, she came to my side while the others were out of hearing. "Hello, Steve. What do you think?"

I thought of the beach, of catching her as she falls, laughing, helping her to her feet, hearing her lilt and her name for the first time. "I don't know. What do you think?"

She looked down the length of the hot tub and up its steep, curving walls. The midnight sun gleaming in the glass might cook a man in the cold. "I'm out of my depth. I design astrophysical experiments for space missions. This..." She turned to me, more perplexed than I'd ever known her. "This is your area."

"I explain relativity to people who can't operate a voice interface."

"No, you generate bold ideas." Without bothering to see if anyone was watching, she set her gloved hand on my parka-covered chest. "And you love me."

"That died long ago."

"Does it still hurt?"

I stepped back. Her hand fell away. "You know it does."

"Ergo, it's not dead. If it was, it wouldn't. Q.E.D." It could have been a joke, but no humor flickered in her eyes. "Steve. The top brains are at work on this. Academia, military, cyberbusiness. Fame, fortune, and power are buried here." She stomped a foot on the glass. It deflected the force without effort. "But no one has a clue. I need you."

"It always came down to that, didn't it?"

She turned sharply and waved a hand over her head. "All in, folks! Time for cocoa!"

The real scientists returned. She led us out of the hot tub to the shacks where we would be eating, sleeping, and working for the next few weeks. I brought up the rear, odd man out, the only one not qualified, the only one Iona trusted to find an answer.

Most research begins with the work of others. I read for a whole week. Measurements, experiments, hypotheses formulated and discarded, speculation torn asunder, and from all this one extraordinary fact rose to the surface: the hot tub was so simple as to be meaningless. The rock was just rock, albeit polished to nanometer smoothness. Over it had been laid a transparent cover of such strength that diamond drills couldn't crack it. The substance hadn't been analyzed because no sample could be collected. Spectroscopy proved useless; it neither absorbed nor emitted radiation. Harder than diamond; resistant to acids and other solvents; harboring weak, continuous electromagnetic currents reminiscent of a superconductor…what *was* this stuff? Even stranger, why would anyone bother? For someone clearly had, and it hadn't been us. A lot of eyes would have turned to the stars and wondered, had it not been the season of perpetual day.

Iona spent her time talking with the others and ignoring me. I saw her in passing and at mealtimes, but our eyes never met. Whenever she slipped by, I wished I could follow or that she might at least favor me with a backward glance. But those wishes were folly. There could be no starting over. Ours had never been a reciprocal relationship. She contrived to bring me into her life because she needed my leaps of logic. She offered a trade: my brain for everything she could give, and I unwittingly agreed. I loved it until I didn't, whereupon it proved intolerable.

Eight years, seven months, and twenty-five days later, I had once more played into her hands, only this time I could neither ask for, nor expect, repayment. She knew but offered just the same. That was Iona. Accounts had to balance. Late that night in the kitchen with my laptop, I was falling asleep to the silent drone of another uninspiring research paper while nibbling on a peanut butter sandwich when she slipped into the chair by my side with two glasses and a bottle of cheap red wine. She poured us each a little and slid one at me. She'd never been one for hard liquor. Nor for cheap, but one makes do with what one has.

"Anything?" she asked.

In answer, I closed the laptop and shoved it aside.

She nodded. “I’ve read them all five times, myself. Lots of stuff about how it works. How it doesn’t work, actually.”

“And nothing about what it’s for.”

She smiled at the table. It might have been eight and a half years, but we still knew each other’s thoughts. “I asked myself, what would Steve say about that? Guess what answer I got?”

I propped my tired head on my fist. I had no clue.

She mimicked the action with a little smile. Her exhaustion matched mine. “You ever see one of those archeological digs where they cover the area with a transparency so tourists can see the finds in place?”

“Sure.”

“That’s what I think this is.” Righting herself, she fiddled with her glass. “A window.”

“On a forty-million-year-old dig?”

“Right.” She sipped her wine. “Then you’d ask yourself why.”

Since I didn’t have to, I didn’t.

“Why display a swath of ordinary rock?” She pushed my glass closer to me.

I gave in and accepted it. “And the answer?”

“That’s why you’re here.”

“How the hell should I know?”

We alternately drank and looked into each other’s eyes while the black numbers on the LCD wall clock changed. One minute. Two minutes. Three minutes.

“You will,” she said.

“Iona—“

“What can I give you?”

“I stopped playing that game years ago.”

“Money? An interview?” She winked at me. “Sex? I’m kidding, of course.”

"I don't want anything. I'll come up with some wacky idea, you can take the credit, and I'll go home to the warmth."

She poured more wine for us. "Where is home these days?"

"Connecticut. A town called North Canaan, in the northwest part of the state."

"Why there?"

"It's close enough to my agent and publisher but far enough from New York."

We finished our second glass. She regarded the bottle then pushed it away. "Name anything."

"Except sex."

Rising, she gathered up bottle and glasses. "If you wanted, I could go there."

"Don't."

She shrugged. "You'll figure this out. When you do...anything."

I watched her go, wishing I could name something. And she knew it.

She had jarred my thoughts, anyway. The exact path I walked and the time it took are hazy now, but they ran something like this:

A window.

Onto what? The transparency was fused to the rock. The immense weight of the glacier scraping over it through the ages hadn't scratched it. Nothing would have been visible beneath it forty million years ago that wasn't visible today. Earth rock couldn't be *that* fascinating to an alien race. Geology was geology, no matter the star you orbited.

But Earth was, in fact, different then. The Eocene epoch started out warm and iceless, with forests pole to pole. Toward its end, the planet began to cool. Arctic forests were in transition, plants and animals adapting to the changes. Polar ice formed. Having drawn a long, slow breath, Earth embarked on an equally long, equally slow exhale.

Somewhere, a physician with a stethoscope listened, examined, diagnosed.

Of course.

A window, yes. But not onto rock. Onto the world above.

I sent Iona a text first thing that morning, asking her to meet me in the hot tub, alone, before breakfast. There in our parkas and gloves and goggles, I delivered the insight she wanted.

She stared into the glass below our feet. I could sense tickles of electricity running through it, running through us, but was it real or illusion? Was the cause outside or within us?

"Are they still watching?" she asked.

"*Homo sapiens* has only been on Earth for two hundred thousand years. We're half a percent the age of this thing." I scraped my heel across the surface. It left no mark. "How can we even guess?"

Pensive, she slowly knelt and pressed her insulated palm to the transparency, fingers spread in greeting. It seemed the thing to do, so I joined her. Our hands signaled hello as one, then she took mine in hers and squeezed gently. "How do we evaluate this hypothesis?"

"I don't think we do, Iona. This technology is beyond us. Maybe in a century or three, but not now."

"That isn't the answer I want."

"Sometimes we don't get the answer we want."

She squeezed my hand a bit harder before letting it go. We stood. The sun reflecting in the sleek curve of the walls began to sear us.

"I know," she said. "I'm sorry. For both of us." She motioned toward the exit, and we walked. Emerging from the trench, she paused and looked back. "We could write a paper together. Yes?"

"Is that your offer? My name next to yours?"

She didn't say anything. She didn't have to. Nor did I. We shared another window, one of human origin through which we knew each other's souls. If the view wasn't always pretty, it was at least true.

She slipped her arm through mine. "I'm starving," she said. "Let's make some notes over breakfast."

Miraculous Morgan

I'd grown accustomed to dying. We all do if we live long enough. My latest death, the third in ten months, came over dinner at a chain restaurant with Angela and took the form of, "I'm sorry, I can't watch you do this to yourself, I've met someone else, I'm sorry I'm sorry I'm so, so sorry..."

I should have died and, in the following month or three, decomposed and resurrected. That's the usual process, no? Hell, I was only forty-three and had a few good demises left in me. But the knife had struck too quickly too many times of late: my job axed in a reorganization; my identity stolen and credit profile demolished, making it so impossible to land a new job that I quit trying; and now Angela, who it turned out wasn't a for-better-or-for-worse woman, which fact neither of us knew until then, but that's how we learn, right? By doing our worst.

My friend Ignacy, on the other hand, reveled in worst. Not that he was a holy terror himself. He just loved psychoanalyzing everyone from presidents to street corner beggars, delivering his diagnoses in impeccable English wrapped in a thick Polish accent. Fittingly, I called him "Professor," because he had been in his home country. Arriving on these shores, he traded academia for real estate investment, a.k.a. house flipping. It hadn't made him rich, but he loved it. It gave him so much raw material to work with, be they fellow flippers, buyers, sellers, contractors, agents, lawyers, or inspectors. I met him when I bought a house from him. I stayed in touch because (probably) I had a head full of demons. Two days after Angela, I needed to evict a few of them, so I called him.

"You know what your problem is, Patrick?" he asked after hearing the long version.

"Grief," I told him. "Obviously."

"No. Everybody has that these days. Guess again."

He wasn't much of an explainer. He enjoyed leading patients to their disease. Slowly. Right now, I didn't care to oblige.

"It's not hard to figure," he said once he tired of the silence. "People are like rivers."

"Nobody can step on me the same way twice?" I suggested.

"Don't be an idiot. What does every river need?"

I couldn't see where rivers needed anything. They just were.

"Water, Patrick, water. And you have run dry. *That's* your problem. You just need water."

"I hydrate regularly," I assured him. "So far, it hasn't brought me employment. Or a constant woman."

"I speak metaphorically, of course." Ignacy sounded the way he must have looked when scolding a dull student. "Metaphorical water."

"Great, Professor, just great. Where do I get that? At the metaphorical drinking fountain?"

"Precisely."

Now if only I knew where they kept that hidden. Probably in the same vault as the fountain of youth. "True genius," I said. "Thank you."

"You are most welcome. I will introduce you to her."

"To who?"

"Morgan. Are you free this evening?"

"Morgan?"

"Yes, Morgan. Morgan Morgan. An unusual name, but she is an unusual woman. Are you free this evening?"

"Damn it, Professor, that's the *last* thing I need right now."

He laughed. "You have a one-track mind."

"And it's derailed, I know. Fixing me up with a new woman won't right it."

"She is not precisely new, and I am not fixing you up. I am only saying, she can help you."

"What is she, a retired therapist?"

"No, Patrick. She is a miracle. Once more: are you free this evening?"

I would be free every evening for some time. And while I didn't believe in miracles, Ignacy was nearly impossible to refuse.

We met at a small Mexican restaurant off route one at the north end of Biscayne Bay. Ignacy's lanky form stood guard by the door as I arrived, but he didn't lead me in. Rather, he escorted me like a church usher to open-air seating on the south side of the building, a lush little area surrounded by palms and live oaks and a wrought iron fence. In the lowering sun, a warm spring breeze bearing a faint salt tang rattled the leaves.

For such a fine evening, the tables were strangely empty. One diner alone was present: a dark-eyed woman toying with the strands of her dark hair, her lips upturned in a half-smile, her eyes on something other than us. Those high cheekbones set in a heart-shaped face possessed an ageless quality, as though she'd been waiting breathless at this table her whole life for something wonderful that hadn't yet happened, or maybe that was happening time and again for her amusement.

"Do not say a word," Ignacy whispered, "unless she asks you a question."

"Why not?"

"She is not what she seems."

Not that I knew what she seemed, other than a stunning woman who didn't wish to be disturbed by idiots like us.

Ignacy led me to her table, intent upon disturbing her anyway. "Hello, Morgan," he said with an easy smile. "Thank you for seeing us."

She turned her almost smile on him.

Ignacy pulled out two chairs, motioned me into one, settled easily into the other. He folded his hands on the table. "What's good here?"

"Everything," Morgan breathed as though the restaurant's offerings aroused her. "Pick something at random." She laughed, and only then did I realize she had neither food nor drink nor menu.

Ignacy laughed with her. He pointed at me. "This is Patrick." To me, he said, "Morgan is an executive assistant for a real estate broker of my acquaintance. That is how we met. I know many people, Patrick, but the happiest people I know are those who work in that office. That observation was so striking, I was compelled to investigate."

Of course he was, but he kept his methods and conclusions to himself. Under orders to say nothing, I said nothing. A waitress bounded into the silence, squealing with delight. "Oh my God! Morgan! I haven't seen you for a *month*, girl, whaddaya been up to? Don't tell me, I know! Work, work, work! You don't get a break, do you? Oh, hi, guys." (The last was directed at Ignacy and I.) "What can I get you all to drink?"

"Margaritas all around," Morgan said.

The waitress gave her a pat on the shoulder, which earned her a reciprocal pat on the hand before she skipped off to Oz. Or whatever.

Morgan smiled after her. "Happy girl," she mused. "Funny, she's never told me her name. Isn't that weird? I've known her for over a year." She turned to Ignacy, losing none of her smile. "So why are we here, Iggy?"

I cringed. Had anyone else called him that, he would have erupted like Vesuvius. Morgan must have earned the right somehow, because he didn't even flinch. He spilled out my life story, or the portion I had told him, which I didn't appreciate. Shouldn't that have been my job? Shouldn't I have been allowed the dignity of filtering the details before pouring them into a total stranger's glass?

When the tale was told out, Morgan leaned back, stretched the most beautiful stretch in history, and smiled at the sky. Birds twittered in the trees and traffic rushed by on the road while she said not a word. Ignacy held his breath for over half a minute before, unable to willfully asphyxiate himself, he exhaled and gulped in a lungful of fresh oxygen.

"How do you feel, Patrick?" Morgan asked, at last freeing me to speak.

Alas, I didn't know what to say. How did she *think* I felt?

"Suicidal?"

"*What?* No!"

"Oh, good. You've got that going for you."

I wouldn't have thought of that.

"What else?"

Confusion boiled into anger. Who the hell was this woman? Why should I bare my soul to a secretary, for God's sake, executive or otherwise? "How do you think?" I snapped. "I lost everything in less than a year!"

"Right. And what have you done about it?"

"What am I supposed to do about it?"

Morgan was still smiling, smiling as though I'd said everything's great and I love your hair and your eyes and your mind and your soul and your body and please, please, please would you dance with me? But when she spoke, her words proved strangely pedestrian: "Look for a new job, maybe?"

"I did until I didn't, and since then I haven't, because what's the damn point?"

"Oh, you need a point." She pushed back from the table, but the drinks arrived just then, borne by the giddy waitress who then took our orders—although Ignacy and I hadn't seen a menu, so we followed Morgan's lead and got chiles rellenos—and bounced back to the kitchen.

"Where were we?" Morgan asked herself. "Oh yes, the point." She rose, sashayed to my side, and gazed down on me like an angel descending from heaven. I was jumble of anger, confusion, pain, and more confusion, but somehow she registered none of that. She only saw…

…well, something positive, I guess. I don't know what. I only know what she did.

She took my head in her hands and kissed me on the lips. Hard.

I assume food arrived and we ate before parting company. I guess. I only know that the deep blue of evening had overspread the world when I found myself behind the wheel of my car with Ignacy leaning in the open window, grinning like an idiot. "Are you safe to drive?" he asked.

"I don't know," I said. Streetlights blazed and cars rushed by and the air wrapped us like a warm blanket.

"How do you feel?"

Not bad. Almost good. No, better than good. Clarity dawned in the growing dark, but I was afraid to admit it, because I didn't know what it meant. "I'm okay," I said. "Professor..."

He punched my shoulder. It kind of hurt, but I didn't mind.

"What happened?" I asked. "Why did she…" Or had she? Maybe I dreamed it.

"I told you, Patrick. A miracle. See how tomorrow goes."

He slipped into the night, leaving me to remember how to drive and where I lived and how to get there. Thank God I remembered the GPS.

The next morning, I didn't rise until ten forty-five. I opened my apartment windows to the morning breeze. Over breakfast, I brushed up my résumé and posted it on several job boards. By lunchtime, I had applied to a dozen likely employers, and by evening I had three interviews lined up. Not bad for a day's work. Along the way, I pinged my attorney, who said my credit catastrophe was untangling, albeit at leisure.

I forgot all about Ignacy and Morgan Morgan and chiles rellenos until my cell phone went off at nine that evening while I was lost in a book.

"I assume," Ignacy said when I answered, "that your day went well."

"Why wouldn't it?" I'd meant it as a rhetorical question. Days *should* go well, shouldn't they?

"They have not lately, or so you told me."

"Did I?"

"Do you not recall your many setbacks?"

Oh, sure, I'd had my share of bumps in the road, but…

But…

Wait a minute.

Ignacy laughed. "I told you, my friend. Morgan is a genuine miracle."

Wait a minute.

"Are you still there?"

Where else would I be? "Yesterday I was miserable. Today I'm winning a marathon. What's wrong with me?" The absurdity of the question struck me as soon as I'd uttered it. "I mean, what's right with me?"

"The dry river is filled to its banks once more. That is what she does. She fills you with life."

"How?"

"That, Patrick, is the miracle. I do not think even she knows. Somehow, happiness flows from her being to yours, and you are revived. She has but to touch you, and it is done."

"But Professor, she *kissed* me."

"Studies have confirmed that kissing is a form of touching."

"But *why* did she kiss me?"

"How should I know? Maybe you look like a good kisser. Do not question it. You are on your way again. Mission accomplished. Now I must sleep. Good night!" He disconnected before I could object.

Unfortunately, the question nagged at me until dawn.

You'd think it would be easy to locate a woman named Morgan Morgan. Morgan is a common enough last name. A common enough first name, too. But tautonymously? There couldn't be too many of those. Yet she was a ghost. No social media, no professional listings, no nothing locatable online, and with well over 11,000 real estate agents in Miami, it would take more lifetimes than I had left to cold call them all.

Ignacy, of course, knew her. After last night's send-off, I wasn't sure he'd cooperate, but I texted him anyway.

One does not lead one to a woman like Morgan, he replied.

You did yesterday.

That was an emergency.

So is this.

No, Patrick. This is intrusion.

I'll waste the rest of my life looking if you don't help me find her. I'll be miserable again.

I stand corrected. This is obsession.

Then help me. Please.

He capitulated, with the caveat that he would only arrange a meeting if Morgan agreed. Two hours later, I was planted on a stone bench in Ferré Park overlooking Biscayne Bay at the bottom of the steps leading to the Giant Head Statue, "Looking Into My Dreams, Awilda," by Jaume Plensa, a gleaming forty-foot bust of a woman with eyes closed in serene contemplation. She wasn't Morgan, not by a long shot, yet maybe she was on the inside.

Thirty minutes passed before the woman herself descended the steps from the science and art museums, humming. Traffic buzzed the causeway behind and route one to the west, at the foot of a line of 50-plus story condos and hotels. She wore pale jeans and a yellow t-shirt festooned with bees swarming a honey-laden hive. I still couldn't figure her age. She might have been twenty-one going on fifty, or fifty going on twenty-one. She bore neither the marks of time nor the freshness of youth. She carried herself with confidence, but not quite lightly. If woman is enigma, she was twice a woman.

She sat close beside me, legs crossed at the ankles, and gazed at the seabirds wheeling over the bay. Was she waiting for me to speak? Or should I keep silent until spoken to, as before?

Maybe she heard the thought. "Chatter away," she said.

But once more, I couldn't. I found no words for the thousand questions mobbing my brain.

"Okay," she said. "Let's walk. That might jog something loose."

We strolled down the path close together but not touching, not talking. She gazed upon the water, the birds, the palms and oaks, the city beyond. I kept an eye on my feet. We reached the southern corner of the baywalk, doubled back, then cut west on the tree-lined path into the heart of the park.

Morgan laughed a laugh as bright as the sun. "Hopeless, aren't you?"

"I was better yesterday."

"Life ebbs and flows. Everyone has high-tide days and low-tide days. Or weeks, or months, or sometimes years."

A version of Ignacy's river analogy. Maybe he got it from her. "Even you?" I asked.

She grinned at me. "Nope. Never me."

The path forked, and she veered right. We passed an old couple walking hand-in-hand the other direction, talking in hushed tones. Another right, and we were headed back to the giant head.

"You hit bottom," she said, "things turn around, you get better. Eventually you're on top again. Usually it just happens, but sometimes you need a push. Or a kick in the pants."

"You didn't kick me," I objected.

There was that grin again. It fell somewhere between impish and devilish. "You were too far gone. You needed a transfusion." Morgan suddenly looked up and pointed at the sky. A bald eagle wheeled high on the thermals directly overhead. How had she known it was there? She seemed connected to every living thing around us. We watched it spiral off to the south until it became a dot.

But back to the subject. "How is a kiss a transfusion?" I asked.

"A touch is a transfusion. A kiss is a massive transfusion for stubborn bastards like you." She laughed and poked my shoulder. I felt a flush of warmth, as though the sun had momentarily brightened. She waited for my reaction, her lips drawn into a silent, "Oooo…"

"What the hell did you do?"

"Call it a gift. A dose of life from me to you."

"You mean…" I didn't know what she meant, but somehow something—energy, hope, meaning, something—had flowed into me. Rivers. Tides. Miracles.

Whoa…

But I still couldn't open myself up, not fully, so I fell back on a joke. "Then you're not in the habit of kissing total strangers."

Morgan loved that one. "You sound so disappointed."

That hit too close to the mark. In truth, I wouldn't have minded another one.

"Don't get your hopes up, buddy. You'd probably pass out. And it hurts."

"It didn't hurt," I assured her. Not that I much remembered the moment, but I associated no pain with it.

"Not you. Me."

We were approaching the statue. I stopped dead. She turned, head cocked in amusement. "I hurt you?" I asked.

"Technically, I hurt myself."

"For me. I mean…I didn't ask…hell, now I feel bad. I'm sorry."

"Don't be, Patrick. I did it because I wanted to."

"But why? Why does it hurt? Why would you…" I was sinking back into the dark pit of the day before yesterday. Needing something to hold to, I searched the sky for that eagle, but it was long gone. Since a joke is better than nothing, I took refuge there. "Why the hell are your first and last names the same?"

She laughed. "Blame my father. I'm Morgan Miami Morgan from Miami. That spells *mmmm*. Cute, huh? When I was in high school, I threatened to move to Pittsburgh just to ruin it."

She'd one-upped me. "So back to my question."

"Which was?"

"Damned if I know."

"That's okay, I think I got it. Think of me as a candle."

Another analogy. Maybe I was too literal for all this. Whatever this was. "How so?"

"A candle weeps its life away to shed its light on the world."

"You're too happy to weep. I thought you never had low-tide days."

"I don't, but candles have only so much wax. Every time I give life to someone, I lose a bit of it myself." She drew so close I thought she meant to kiss me again. While I would have loved that, I couldn't allow it, not if what she was saying was true, so I stepped back. She closed in again, eyes sparkling like sapphires. "How old am I?"

Even at intimate range I couldn't tell. I split the difference. "Late thirties?"

"Do I look it?"

"Yes, no, maybe so."

"My body is twenty-seven. My heart? I don't know. Maybe sixty. It's hard to tell."

That calculus horrified me. She'd be dead at forty, if not sooner.

"It's okay, Patrick."

"It's not. You need to stop."

"Stop touching? Stop helping? That would only kill me faster." She smiled as though having one of those low tide moments she refused to admit. "Truth be told, I do sometimes wish I could lie on a beach for a week without feeling anyone's emptiness. But no, I couldn't do that to the rest of the world."

I had a strange urge to protect her. Not that I'd know how. But maybe I could buoy her up. "Morgan Miami Morgan, you're in Miami, not Pittsburgh. Beaches aren't a problem."

That's all it took. She laughed. Her low tides really weren't that low, after all. Maybe if I could keep her laughing, she wouldn't grow old before her time.

"Whoa, down boy. We barely know each other."

I'd forgotten; she had a mystic connection to her surroundings. Of course, she knew my thoughts. "That doesn't mean I don't like you." Turnabout being fair play, I poked *her* in the shoulder. That ought to be safe. She hadn't touched me, after all. I'd touched her.

But it happened anyway, only this time it felt different. I suffered a moment of disorientation and nearly lost my balance.

Morgan gasped, wide-eyed, lips parted in astonishment. She had felt it, too. "What did you do?" she sputtered.

"I don't know. This." Fearing the result but needing to find out, I touched my fingertip to her shoulder.

There it was again, a dizziness that passed as quick as it came.

She sucked in a breath and muttered, "Whoa."

Stupidly, I examined my fingertip. Whatever this was, it wasn't like when she touched me. Not for me, not for her. It was…

…backwards!

"You have it, too," she whispered.

I did. Somehow, I did. But what was *it*?

"The gift," Morgan explained. "The miracle. I gave you a bit of life, and you gave it back. Did you know you could do that?"

I shook my head. It had never happened before, not that I ever noticed. And I would have noticed.

"I have to know," she said. She snatched up my hand and squeezed, and I squeezed back, and we looked at our entwined fingers as a sensation like the tide rising and falling, rising and falling, flowed back and forth between our bodies.

We let go.

We looked at our own hands and each other's hands and our own hands.

"You want to lie on a beach?" I asked.

"I do. I absolutely do."

I kissed her cheek, just to feel some of that life flow back to her. It didn't quite hurt and only diminished me a little. I was still more alive than she had found me, and she was more alive than I had left her.

"Then guess what," I said, forcing the words through my tingling lips. "You're stuck with me."

Solve This

Two things caught Detective Sergeant William Caldicott's attention. First, a puff of musty wind escaped from an old house whose windows and doors, shuttered for a decade, had suddenly been thrust open. And that was strange because this stretch of the riverbank was devoid of homes. The land rose from the pebble-strewn shore to a gravel road that hugged the base of a thirty-foot slope awash in ankle-high grasses and shaggy stalks crowned with tiny flowers of red, yellow, and blue. Across the river, a state highway passed behind broken stands of oak and maple in full summer leaf. This was farmland lightly sprinkled with factories. What had birthed that breeze?

But it passed quickly as it came, leaving Caldicott's second and more significant observation: the corpse on the shore.

The patrol officers had already closed the gravel road two hundred feet north and south of the body. Caldicott parked at the north blockade and walked in. Even from the road, certain details were clear. The deceased was female, age around sixty. Sprawled face down, head and chest in the water, her graying hair was feathered in the current, tracing its flow as iron filings trace a magnetic field. She wore nearly spotless charcoal jeans and a white cotton T-shirt. No holes, no blood, no spatters of mud. Not the least sign of struggle. She might have had a heart attack while on hands and knees drinking from the water.

Two techs moved carefully about the body in a measured dance. A sandy-haired young man named Sam photographed the scene while his colleague Carly, a slightly older redhead, snooped for collectable evidence. Caldicott examined the slope from road to beach but saw no sign of the deceased's passing. The ground was too rocky to collect footprints, the slope too gradual to trigger rockslides. He left the road and gingerly approached the body. "Anywhere I shouldn't step?" he called.

Carly waved him down.

Caldicott circled them, not getting in the way, not seeing anything he hadn't seen from above. "ID?" he asked.

"Nothing, sir," Carly replied. "No purse, nothing in her pockets."

He bent down, hands on knees, and examined the side of the deceased's face. Her makeup, except where smudged by the water, looked so pristine she might have been going to the opera. "The ambulance should be here in a few minutes," he said. "When you're done, let's get her out of the water." He stood and looked north. The officers there leaned on their cars, waiting, talking, probably occupied with baseball and summer vacations.

"That's it," Carly said.

They drew the body from the water and turned it over. The photographer documented what they saw, which was nothing, really: a Mediterranean face that reminded Caldicott of a perfect olive, dark eyes, no trauma. Had she sat up, he wouldn't have been surprised.

An ambulance trundled in from the north. One of the officers stationed there motioned it through. Only when it cleared the patrol cars did Caldicott notice someone had followed it, a woman now standing motionless beside a black Camry parked just beyond the squads.

The officers spotted her at the same time. One approached and briefly conversed with the woman before coming halfway down the road, where he called to Caldicott. "Lady up here wants to see you. Says she has information."

Incredible timing, Caldicott thought. He didn't trust coincidences. "Send her down."

The officer motioned the woman through and rejoined his interrupted baseball—or whatever—conversation.

She trekked the gravel road as though born to it, crunching along in a pair of white walking shoes. Like the deceased, she had a Mediterranean look: that dark, wavy hair fluttering in the wind, those dark eyes, that face like an olive. Thirty at most, she must be the dead woman's little sister. She stood but five feet tall in a long, ivory dress too formal for the landscape and her footwear. When she arrived, Caldicott towered over her, but her eyes betrayed no smallness.

"You're Caldicott?" she asked.

"That's right. Who are you?"

"Velia Solano."

Caldicott had never heard the name before. He thought he should have. Someone mixed up in murder ought to have caught his attention somewhere along the line. He gazed at the body on the shore, now being bagged. Velia watched, too, clouded, confused.

"You have information?" Caldicott prompted.

"Yes. No. That is…" She watched the paramedics load the body into the ambulance. As the doors closed, she squeezed her eyes shut.

"Take your time. Do you know her? A relative? A friend?" Or rival or enemy or any combination thereof. All he needed was a name, one he knew, one stashed away in his personal files.

She didn't supply it. Across the river, birds flitted among the trees dotting the shore while a turkey vulture soared on the thermals. A truck rattled by on the state highway. "I need your help."

"I thought you had information."

"Not to give. To trade. I need to know who did this and why."

He scratched a line in the rocky soil with his heel.

Velia squirmed under his severe gaze. "I at least need assurances. You'll think I'm involved."

"Are you?"

Her mouth twitched.

Caldicott figured that meant yes. "Why are you here, ma'am?"

"I—" She looked away, unwilling or unable to look him in the eye. "I told you. I need to know who killed…" She nodded toward the ambulance. "And why."

Was her discomfort real or a cover? Or had she wandered out of a nearby group home?

The ambulance trundled onto the gravel road. Velia watched it go, as pale as if she'd seen a ghost. As if she was the ghost.

"Do you live around here?" Caldicott asked.

She shook her head. "I spend my life on the road."

"Doing what?"

"Historical research."

So not just a nutcase. A smart one. The worst kind. "How about you tell me what you know so I can do my job."

The ambulance vanished over a rise. Velia wiped away a few tears and nodded.

"So?"

"I only know what I heard on the news."

Caldicott couldn't recall any news big or small, that could be connected to this. "Which was?"

"I was poisoned and dumped here. You found my purse up the hill." She pointed.

The first-person pronouns cinched it. She was off her rocker. "We didn't find any purse, ma'am."

"You will if you look."

That gave him two choices. Either they needed to find the facility from which she had escaped, or she was indeed connected. All he needed to know was whether a purse was hidden in the grass.

He told her to wait and tramped off to find out. As on the shore, he found no sign of anyone passing. No footprints. Nothing trampled. Yet three quarters up the hill, almost directly above the position of the body, he came upon a glossy black purse, slightly battered with age, the shoulder strap trailing downhill.

The techs on the shore and the officers blocking the road watched, no doubt wondering what the hell he was doing up there. He waved the techs up and showed them the find. While they went to work, he marched downhill to Velia.

"How did you know?" he asked.

"I told you. It was on the news."

"Wrong answer. I only just found it. How did you know?"

She pinched her lips and looked to the river again. "I told you you'd think I was involved."

"Give me a reason not to."

She looked to be wrestling with her conscience. Her voice dropped to a whisper. "You can't tell anyone."

"You don't dictate terms, ma'am."

"Then I won't tell you anything." She turned to go.

Caldicott allowed her a few steps. "I have probable cause to detain you."

Velia stopped without looking back. "Like what?"

"Like you knowing a detail that hasn't been released. You either witnessed what happened here or you participated in it."

She turned on him, furious. "Of *course* I participated in it! I *died*!"

The nearest mental facility wasn't exactly within walking distance. Caldicott wondered how Velia got here. Or maybe she had only just crossed into madness, pushed by witnessing whatever had happened. "You have ID?" he asked.

Up the hill, Carly waved a large evidence bag containing a black object and started down.

Velia looked put out but no longer enraged. "In my car."

"Get it. Don't run off."

She hurried to her Camry and returned shortly with a shiny black purse. She dug out her driver's license and presented it to Caldicott as Carly arrived and handed him the evidence bag. Inside nestled the same shiny black purse, slightly less worn, and its contents, including a driver's license. Caldicott compared Velia's license to the one in the bag, then returned the evidence to Carly and told her she could go.

Once the tech was out of range, he asked, "Which is the fake?

"Neither."

"Same name, same address, same number, but different photos and expiration dates. One of them has to be fake."

Velia drew close and whispered. "Please believe me. She was me, only older. I don't know what happened. I don't know who did it or why. All I know is, after I leave today, thirty-one years pass before I end up right back here, at this moment, and die by someone's hand." She shuddered and squeezed her purse to her chest. "I told you, I do historical research. I must have uncovered someone's dirty secret, and they silenced me. But all I know is what I heard on the news tomorrow."

Aside from being absurd, it was interesting speculation. "You mentioned poison," Caldicott prompted. "How could you know that?"

"It was reported."

Reported. Tomorrow. Right. "What kind of poison?"

"Botulinum toxin."

He wouldn't have expected that. Pranksters usually claimed cyanide or arsenic or strychnine. "And you heard that on the news."

She nodded and stepped back. "I have to go now."

"I don't want you wandering off. You either need help or you're neck-deep in this. Probably both."

Velia bit her lip. "Just solve this. You see that over there?" She pointed to the shore, now devoid of activity.

Caldicott looked but saw nothing he hadn't already seen. "No," he said and turned back to find Velia gone, a wisp of smoke on the wind. She wasn't on the road, wasn't up the hill, wasn't along the riverbank. Even her car had vanished, although she couldn't have reached it so fast.

Probably he'd never see her again, which ordinarily would be a good thing. He could do without the crazy. But that still left him with two copies of the same purse, two nearly identical driver's licenses, and potential botulism poisoning.

And, if Velia wasn't mad, two copies of the same woman in the same place and time.

It was going to be one of those weeks.

"Too melodramatic."

The assessment, rendered by Detective Hope Satterleigh, was delivered with a finality that defied objection. Caldicott would have agreed had he not seen Velia Solano's tricks with purses and licenses, not to mention her vanishing act. How had she *done* that?

Standing with her at the edge of their cramped office, where a folding table next to a sink served as a coffee station, Caldicott watched Satterleigh pull the pot from the ancient office coffee maker and swirl the dark liquid. She peered at it with a scientific scowl. Maybe she'd spotted some new life form evolving in it.

"Dirty secrets," she muttered. "Claiming to be dead. Hell." She poured a mug of coffee and spooned in enough sugar to thicken it.

Caldicott grimaced at the results. "I know. But we have to take her seriously. She was right about the purse and the cause of death. Wacko, maybe, but she's involved."

Swallowing a gulp of the alleged coffee, Satterleigh grimaced, too. "Needs more sugar." Without acting on her own suggestion, she stepped to the end of the table and leaned against the dingy white wall. "You ever hear of Capgras syndrome?"

"Isn't that when you're convinced a friend has been replaced by someone else?"

She nodded. "This is that, only backwards. Solano's convinced the corpse replaced *her*. Doesn't mean she's not also the killer, of course. We ever have a nut job like that around here?"

Caldicott shoved his hands in his pockets while Satterleigh took another gulp of her coffee. She might be young, but she ought to know

Jackson County better. For nearly two decades, Caldicott had bent his skills to the study of the county's people, noting, memorizing, recording, and Satterleigh hadn't escaped his scrutiny. She only had to consider herself to answer her own question. She leaned against the wall, tall, thin, smug, dark eyes piercing everything but perceiving not half enough. She was a good detective but surprisingly naive.

"Everyone's off their rocker in some way," he said.

Satterleigh laughed. "Yeah? What's your psychosis?"

He wasn't about to tell her *that*, but he had a ready answer. "Probably that when a woman says she's been murdered, I don't automatically write it off as nonsense."

"That sure qualifies. So, the driver's license address. Does old, dead Velia live there, or young, looney Velia?"

"Neither, anymore. It's a farmhouse on the southern edge of the county, owned by an older couple. They rent out two rooms, usually to migrants. The deceased Solano rented one of them for seven months. A week ago, she settled up and left without saying where she was going. They haven't seen her since."

"Ran off with those dirty secrets, huh?

"Maybe. Homicide by poison tends to be premeditated. She likely got under somebody's skin. Anyway, I'll be talking to their other boarder tomorrow. He was out when I dropped by."

Satterleigh regarded the remains of her coffee, then dumped it in the sink. While she washed out the mug, she said, "Nobody around here could be *that* desperate."

"Sure they could."

"Like who? We're just farms and a fistful of small towns."

Caldicott figured she could use a wake-up call. In a whisper so nobody would overhear, he said, "Maybe you. How far would you go to avoid gossip about your latest bedfellow?"

Her eyes widened, sparkling with amusement, not fear, not embarrassment.

"A rich, slick attorney, handsome, married to your high school rival. Bit of a thrill, I expect. The payback. The danger. But you wouldn't want word getting out."

"I couldn't care less," she whispered back, none too convincingly.

"Until his wife comes after you with a double-bladed axe."

Satterleigh waved that off. "She's a wimp."

"Point is, cows may outnumber humans here, but the humans have plenty of secrets, some very much worth hiding."

"Affairs probably aren't what Solano had in mind."

Maybe she was being willfully obtuse. He shouldn't have hit so close to home. "Okay. History lesson. Ten years ago, we had a county council comprised of half embezzlers and half extortionists. When their misdeeds blew up in their faces, most of them landed in prison. A couple wormed their way out on technicalities and are still plying their trades in the private sector. Suppose Solano dug up some new dirt on one of them?"

"Sounds like you already have it," Satterleigh said, deadpan.

Well of course he did, but she wouldn't know about that. Nor would she know about his next example, although she should. It was as close to home as her affair. "Fifteen years back there was a county judge named Perry. Any good-looking woman standing trial in Judge Perry's courtroom had a great chance of acquittal. If she agreed to meet him in a motel room before the trial, she was off the hook. We caught him, along with two hotshot lawyers who took kickbacks in exchange for steering female clients his way. One more was hiding in the woodpile, but we could never prove his involvement. Maybe Solano found the evidence."

Satterleigh put up a hand to stop him. "Fine, I'm an idiot. We'll be focusing on past scandals, then?"

"Possibly. She said she does historical research." Leaving the coffee concession—such as it was—they wound their way through the cubicles to Caldicott's desk.

"So, try this on for size," Satterleigh said. "You've got her in two places and two different ages at the same time. Maybe she's a time traveler and her historical research is about our scandal-ridden jurisdiction." She nudged him. "Think what CNN would do with *that*."

"I'd rather not," he said. He sat and logged onto his computer.

In a whisper once more, she said, "Then think about who has the biggest, baddest secrets to hide. I guess I'm off the hook, huh? Screwing a married guy can't possibly top the list."

Caldicott doubted it was that simple, but to avoid compromising his investigation he said. "I guess you are."

Half an hour north of Benton, the county seat, an old farmhouse's windows glowed pale yellow long into the black night. Within, a detective sifted through boxes of unofficial records, seeking answers.

Detective Sergeant William Caldicott had bought this place at auction sixteen years ago after his wife Denise left him for a college professor two states away. He'd never figured out how she had met the bastard, much less how they had carried on a ten-month affair without his knowing. She sprang it on him from the safety of a cell phone two hundred miles away, leaving him with nothing, not even a chance to ask why. And because her ghost haunted every room, every closet, even every cobweb in the house they had shared for over a decade, he dumped it and moved here with nothing but an old oak tree in the front, chestnut and mulberry behind, an old barn out back, and fields of wheat, corn, and soybeans all about for company. And no visitors, ever.

In the silence, his mind picked at the threads, trying to figure it out. A detective ought to be able to figure it out. He replayed his memories of Denise, their chance meeting at the county fair, their whirlwind romance, their agreements and disagreements, fights and lovemaking, but her infidelity remained shrouded in mystery. He read psychology, studied secrecy, deception, and betrayal, pulled examples from history and current events, sought to wedge her into the maze of darkness that ensnared communities, states, countries, the whole world. He discovered underground rivers of lies and dark secrets trickling all through Jackson County. Sometimes he followed them to bring criminals to justice, but of Denise's great crime he found not even a drop of reason.

Eventually, he stopped caring.

By then, Caldicott had acquired another addiction. He popped guilty secrets for breakfast, lunch, and dinner. He became a snake, slithering through the grasses, sniffing, licking, gathering in all his senses detected, delighting in the flavor of other people's sins. He boxed up and stashed away enough material to convict half the county on either moral or legal grounds. He knew the shapes and lengths of all his neighbor's shadows.

Therefore, he must know Velia Solano, who had killed her, and why. Or at least his files knew. He but needed to sift them.

So he did, all through the night. She proved as elusive as Denise. Then again, if guilty secrets had been the motive, there were no shortage of suspects.

"Drop it, Hope. It's ancient history. Nobody cares anymore."

But Detective Hope Satterleigh had Jared Winslow right where she wanted him—naked beneath her nakedness with the air stirred by a slow ceiling fan caressing them—and wasn't about to drop it. He couldn't do anything about it, either. He wanted her there, too. His fingers clung desperately to her, his body moved in time with hers, his voice strained with desire.

Still, the question bothered him, and she wondered why. "I can't, Jared. The boss all but accused you."

Winslow sucked in a sharp breath, then ran a finger down her spine and smirked. "How?"

"He knows you're a lawyer. He knows who your bitch of a wife is. And he brought up Judge Perry."

"I wasn't involved in that. And don't call Sylvia a bitch."

Sylvia had flown to the west coast that afternoon to visit family and would be gone for a week. Now it was two in the morning, and her husband and his mistress had already spent hours making the most of her absence.

"Why not?" Satterleigh asked. "Isn't that why you're *here*?" She thrust down on him for emphasis.

"No, I'm only *here*—" He returned the favor. "—because you can't keep your hands off me."

She didn't take offense. They'd played that game before, each denying interest, each attributing their desire to the other. But she couldn't let him off the hook. "Liar. I dug out the files. The only reason you weren't disbarred and jailed is none of your clients would talk."

"They had nothing to talk about. Why're you harping on it, anyway, and during our recreation time?"

She slipped her arms behind him and rested her head on his shoulder. "Maybe I like it when you squirm. So, what did you do to keep them quiet?"

Winslow's jaw tightened and he dug his fingernails into Satterleigh's arms. She winced but he couldn't see it, and she allowed him no other sign that it hurt. "I mean it, Hope. Drop it. As of now, the subject is off limits."

She breathed in his ear, slow, gentle, until he eased up, then she rolled off him and flopped on her back. They watched the shadowy blades of the ceiling fan turn. "I don't care," she finally said. "It's a turn-on. I know I'm banging a devil, and I like it. But William knows, too, and that could be a problem. If you'd confide in me, maybe I could keep him off your back."

Winslow rolled onto his side. In the dark, he couldn't see more than her outline, yet she felt he was scrutinizing every detail of her face for lies. "Why? Don't tell me you love me?"

"Don't be gross. I love the wickedness and the danger and knifing your bitch-wife in the back."

He crawled on top of her, forced his legs between hers, and pinned her wrists to the bed. His weight pressed her into the mattress. She could barely breathe, much less move. "I said, don't call her that."

"Yeah? Or what?" Her tone was defiant, but she couldn't keep a quiver from her voice. He had never treated her this rough before.

He set his right hand to her throat and squeezed. She gagged and grabbed at his wrist with her free arm, but he was too strong and she couldn't free herself. Panic overtook her. She bucked and slapped at him while the darkness glowed red before her eyes. And then the pressure was gone. He was gone. She gulped down air and rolled over, coughing and sputtering.

The nightstand lamp snapped on, momentarily blinding her. When her eyes adjusted, she found him standing by the bed, pants already on, shaking the wrinkles out of his shirt. He glanced over his shoulder. "Any more questions?"

A million, Satterleigh thought. But she didn't ask a one of them.

Dark clouds scudded overhead as Caldicott pulled into the gravel drive, rocks crunching under his tires. Inside the well-maintained gray farmhouse, a shadow moving across the kitchen window paused to look out. The old couple who lived here, Tom and Angie Claymore, were expecting him. He'd called ahead and asked them to see that their boarder, Juan Garza, stayed put.

Cladicott turned off the car, got out, and shoved the door shut. The dull thud echoed off the farmhouse, the big detached garage, and the barn. The effect was oddly like thunder echoing in the distance. Walking to the front door, he breathed in the warm morning air and soaked up the quiet. He knew next to nothing about these people, and that was somehow comforting. They were like the land on which they lived: remote, still, pure. He didn't need to unearth their secrets; what secrets could they possibly have buried?

Angie was waiting at the door for him and greeted him in a thin, quiet voice. "Mr. Garza is waiting in the living room."

"Thank you, Mrs. Claymore. We'll go for a walk so we don't disturb your morning."

"Not much disturbs me." She smiled a crooked smile. "I don't hear so good anymore, and I hate wearing those annoying hearing aids."

Caldicott returned the smile. "Nevertheless," he said, "we'll talk outside."

She motioned him through to the living room. Juan Garza was seated ramrod straight, hands folded in his lap as though waiting his turn for a job interview or to give testimony. He was dressed in a white button-down shirt and a pair of new jeans and had a two-day growth of stubble on his face.

Caldicott introduced himself and suggested they talk outside. Garza mumbled his consent and followed the detective. As they crunched up the drive toward the barn, Caldicott began, "I assume you knew Velia Solano."

"Yes, sir, a little. We both ate meals with Mr. and Mrs. Claymore." He had a modest accent, but his English pronunciation was good enough. Caldicott figured he was second-generation.

"What can you tell me about her?"

"Not much. She was a professor, I think. Nice lady. Pretty."

Something in Garza's tone suggested he knew Solano better than he admitted. "Did you sleep with her?"

Garza laughed. "Why do you guys always think that? She was too old for me, man."

"She was still breathing, wasn't she?"

"Hey, come on."

"Why do you say she was a professor?"

Garza scratched his cheek. "She said she was doing research."

"What kind?"

They reached the barn, stopped, gazed up at its deteriorating roof. Some of the shingles lay cockeyed. Others had gone missing. Caldicott supposed the structure would need to be razed before long.

"I don't remember," Garza said.

"It might have gotten her killed."

The other shuffled his feet and continued his inspection of the barn roof.

"You sure you didn't sleep with her?"

Garza scratched his cheek again. "Of course, I'm sure."

"What, then?"

"We had a complicated relationship, okay?"

"I think I can handle it. Fill me in."

"She was smart. As smart as I am dumb." Garza practically spat the words out, eyes narrowed in irritation. "My mother wanted me to stay in school, but I didn't. I hated school. I just wanted to party. Stupid, huh?"

"Yeah," Caldicott agreed. "But you're not the only one who ever made that mistake. What's it got to do with Solano?"

"Somehow we started talking. She asked me questions and told me to ask her questions. I told her I was too stupid to even know what to ask. She didn't like it when I said things like that. She kept telling me I wasn't dumb, I just needed a chance to learn. She was like a mom and a teacher and a cheerleader rolled into one. I didn't feel so stupid when I was with her."

Caldicott waited for Garza to continue, but he stood there shaking his head at the barn. Finally, the detective asked, "When was the last time you saw her?"

Garza wandered to the barn and pushed the door open just far enough to look inside. "Last night. She said it was the last time we'd see each other, and she wanted me to know she believed in me. She made me promise to take some classes at the community college." He looked over his shoulder at Caldicott. "I'm not sure I can keep that promise."

"Why not?"

"I'm afraid."

"Of what?"

Looking into the barn again, Garza shuddered. "Failure. I don't guess you've ever had that problem, though."

Denise had proved him a far greater failure than any high school dropout. "You're lying," Caldicott snapped. "Velia Solano spent last night in the morgue."

"I told you it was complicated."

Complicated, hell! The body. Velia pleading to learn her killer's identity. The purses and drivers' licenses and news reports and Botulinum toxin. "Spell it out for me."

"It's like..." Garza leaned against the barn door, suddenly weary. "You know how you know a girl in high school, then you go different directions and you never see her again until thirty years later when you meet her by accident? At first you don't recognize her, then you find her in her eyes, her mouth, her voice, and you know it's her, but she's older, different, because she's lived so many things, all of which have changed her. She's two different people, one you remember, the other you see now, but deep inside they're one."

"You're saying you knew Solano when she was younger."

"No! And yes! I knew her old and young both at the same time. Now she's dead and alive both at the same time. I don't know how. I just know it's true. Because those eyes, that voice, it's her, one woman in two bodies."

It made zero sense but for one thing: it matched Caldicott's experience. "What was she a professor of, Juan?"

"History."

"What was she researching?"

Garza sighed. "Look — "

"Just answer the damn question."

He punched the barn and winced. "Corruption in the legal system."

"In Jackson County?"

"Yeah."

"Why? We're nowhere important." Which was both true and false. His private files testified to that.

Garza fixed Caldicott with a glare. "She had a cousin, railroaded by cops, betrayed by her lawyer, raped by the judge. Figure out the rest yourself. Cop." He stomped back to the house without waiting for a reply.

Caldicott gazed after him. "Hell," he muttered. Hope had been right. A time traveler, however that could happen, and not just a time traveler. A time traveler bent on revenge. Did she hope to uncover the truth and bring the guilty parties to justice, or did she have darker plans?

And if the latter, could even death stop her?

"Velia Solano's cousin was one of Judge Perry's victims." Caldicott had stopped for a cheeseburger on the way back to HQ and picked up one for Satterleigh. But rather than bring it inside, he called and told her to meet him for lunch in his car.

A weird request but Satterleigh complied since free food was involved. Unwrapping her sandwich, she said, "So you think she's after the lawyer."

"I think she's after *your* lawyer, Hope. What the hell happened to your neck?"

She had inspected the small bruises in the mirror before leaving for work that morning. They hadn't seemed that noticeable. "Rough sex. He got a little carried away." She laughed, or tried to.

Caldicott didn't. "You didn't tell him what I said, did you?"

She ate and shook her head without looking at him. He was too good at reading faces.

"Damn it, Hope."

Way too good. "I'll break it off, okay? He crossed a line."

"What, by threatening to kill you? Thank God you know where the line is."

It was like talking to her father. "Drop the sarcasm. Let's focus on the case. Who's Solano's cousin?"

Caldicott didn't answer at once. He took a few bites of his sandwich and washed it down with a gulp of soda. "Eight women testified against Perry and their lawyers. Two others swore out complaints but weren't put on the stand. She must be someone else, someone who didn't come forward. Perry was at it for eight years, so there probably are no shortage of candidates."

Satterleigh could tell he was refusing to look at her. They'd worked together long enough that she knew his moods and signs. "But you know who it is anyway."

"I know who her lawyer was, which narrows it down a bit."

"Jared?"

"Damn straight."

Satterleigh felt like she'd swallowed a rock instead of fast food. Not that there was much difference. "Why?"

"You don't think we tried to interview his clients? Of course, we did. Three of them. Not one would talk, but they couldn't hide their fright. Not from me." Without looking, Caldicott pointed to the marks on Satterleigh's neck. "Plus, I've seen those before. Guess where."

She had no reason to defend Winslow, but she felt compelled to object, if only to save what little dignity she had left. "Any man with hands of similar size could have — "

"Don't be a moron, Hope."

She shoved a bunch of fries into her mouth.

Caldicott sighed. "Are you that much in denial?"

"No. Jared's a self-obsessed bully. But you're talking murder. He wouldn't — "

"The hell he wouldn't. He beat his first wife within an inch of her life."

Satterleigh nearly choked. "*First* wife?"

Caldicott dug through his fries, pulled out a couple, then shoved them back into the holster. "Her name was Carolyn. I'll spare you most of the details. When they found her naked and unconscious in an alley behind a hotel in Baltimore—"

"Baltimore!"

"Yes, Baltimore. When they found her, they didn't think she'd live. They have a top-notch shock trauma center there, though, and they pulled her through. Nobody knew who she was at the time. She had no ID and gave them a fake name. She said she was a tourist from Canada and had been mugged. She contacted a friend in Toronto who flew down and took her 'home.'"

"Does Sylvia know about this?"

Caldicott shook his head, still refusing to look at Satterleigh.

No, Sylvia wouldn't. She was too naive, Jared too slippery. "So how do *you* know all this?"

Caldicott shifted uncomfortably. "How did I know you were sleeping with him? Gossip. Rumor. Public records. Social media. On-site research as needed." He tapped his temple. "And a healthy dose of logic."

That rock in her stomach gained weight. "You *spied* on us?"

Caldicott didn't answer.

"Bastard. You better not have videos."

He turned on her, half angry, half disappointed. Satterleigh had no idea what that meant. Had she hit the mark or missed it by a mile?

"Show me what you've got on us," she said.

"Hope — "

"Show me. Now!"

Caldicott exhaled. "It's no wonder he tried to kill you," he muttered.

"Oh, is that what you're going to do?"

"Not if you're lucky." But the look on his face suggested murder wasn't beyond him.

He slammed the car into gear and drove in silence to his remote farmhouse, a place Satterleigh knew about but had never seen before. It had a forlorn look about it, as though it had stood empty for a century, old and weathered about the edges although not in disrepair. Caldicott parked and led her into the kitchen, where an ancient oak table filled one end of the room and outdated white appliances the other. "Wait here," he said.

She sat at the table while sounds of shoving and shuffling filtered in from the back of the house. Caldicott returned and dropped a stack of binders on the table. "Have fun," he said and went to make coffee.

Satterleigh opened the top binder and leafed through the contents: news clippings, copies of police and court documents, website screen prints, and hand-written notes, all pertaining to the Judge Perry case. Not a word was about her and Winslow, but she worked through it anyway. He delivered her a cup of coffee, then a refill, and an hour later she pushed aside the mass of documents and shook her head.

"Damn, William. This is…" She didn't know what it was, truth be told. "Thorough."

"Yes," he said as though it were nothing.

"Illegal, too, some of it. Some of these documents you shouldn't have here. Or some of the notes. You *have* been spying on people."

"If you want to call it that."

"That's what it is. Why are you doing this?"

"Why are you screwing Jared Winslow?" Caldicott lifted his cup and looked at her over the rim before taking a drink.

That was unfair, if only because she had no answer. She flipped back and forth between several sheets of information. "You have enough here to convict him."

"If only it was admissible in court."

Caldicott said earlier that Winslow had three clients who were likely Judge Perry's victims. Satterleigh leafed through the pages until she found them. All were young, pretty, and charged with jailable offenses. All were acquitted. Caldicott had collected full biographies on them, following them from birth through their appearances in Perry's court and after. There were a lot of gaps, but on the whole they didn't look too remarkable for women who had landed on the wrong side of the law.

Except for one thing.

Maria Regio, the youngest of the three, arrested at age twenty-two, acquitted just seven months before Perry himself was arrested, dead by her own hand at age twenty-four.

Satterleigh pushed the material to her boss. "This is her?"

"I expect so," Caldicott said. "Winslow probably threatened to kill her if she talked. We pushed the opposite direction." He shoved the binder away as though it were poison. "Together, we killed her."

"You think Velia Solano the elder found out about Jared and went after him."

"Yes."

"So why is she running around young again?"

Caldicott rose and took his mug to the sink to rinse it out.

Satterleigh figured she was on her own where that question was concerned. It couldn't possibly have an answer, leastwise no coherent one. But another question, a sword poised at Caldicott's neck, certainly did. She didn't voice it. She didn't need to. He must have considered it.

If Maria Regio, trapped between Jared Winslow and the police, had been driven to suicide, would Velia Solano seek vengeance only on the lawyer, or would she go after the police as well?

Put another way, had she approached Caldicott for help, or to kill him?

An early morning following a sleepless night spent digging through all those binders and boxes and files without finding one damn thing. Detective Sergeant William Caldicott watched the sun rise through his east-facing kitchen window while his coffee cooled on the table beside his folded hands.

Velia Solano, time traveler.

Right.

His morning mental fog slowly burned off. If time travel technology existed, it would be the most powerful weapon ever created, top secret, heavily guarded, probably not even much used lest the secret be stolen. So how did Solano get her hands on it?

More to the point, why did Caldicott even consider such a ludicrous idea? It was a hoax, a sick joke perpetrated with identical purses and fake IDs. Neither he nor Juan Garza had seen one woman of two different ages at the same time. They were two different women, probably related, possibly not one Velia Solano between them. Probably they were both fake identities, since Solano the younger had directed Caldicott to the purse that ID'd Solano the elder.

But the backstory, at least, was real. Judge Perry and Jared Winslow both breathed real air, to the great misfortune of the world, and Maria Regio reposed in the earth. Alias or no, blood or sentiment bound the living Solano to Regio, and desire for revenge filled her heart.

But who was the dead Solano? The case hinged on knowing that, and Caldicott had no clue.

But he knew who did.

Jared Winslow's office in the firm of Drake, Winslow, and Chalmers occupied a large corner of the third floor of a new white stone building at the intersection of Main and First. Although not marble, the structure faked it well, sparkling in the warm morning sun. Caldicott showed up without an appointment, flashed his badge, and brushed by the protesting secretary. Winslow was on the phone when the detective shoved open the door and barged in.

"Call them back," he said loud enough to be heard on the other end of the line.

Winslow blinked. "Sorry, Chuck," he told the receiver. 'Something just came up. Give me an hour, okay? Great, thanks." He hung up and leaned back, hands comfortably folded on his lean abdomen. "William. What an unexpected pleasure."

Caldicott helped himself to one of the big leather guest chairs before the mahogany desk. Behind Winslow, a large window overlooked the town and the cumulus clouds drifting by. "I hear you've had your hands all over my assistant."

With a smirk, Winslow utterly failed to deny it. "You're not her father, are you? I didn't think you and Denise had any children."

Hot anger crashed over Caldicott, but he refused to allow that wave to carry him out to sea. He knew how Winslow worked. He'd watched the lawyer cross-examine prosecution witnesses and had himself been on the receiving end more than once.

"Nope, you didn't. And Hope's a big girl. She can sleep with whoever she wants, can't she?"

"Until they threaten to murder her. Then I take a professional interest."

Winslow examined his nails. "I'm no murderer, William."

"You could be. We have a body in the morgue, and you're at least a person of interest in the investigation. I'd love to make you a full-blown suspect."

"And the accused. And the convicted. What, did I once scare away a fish you were about to catch?"

The game was already old. Caldicott fixed him with a hard stare. "It's what you've done to your clients. And maybe to Velia Solano."

A flock of sparrows flitted by the window, drawing Winslow's attention for a moment. When he turned back, he was all innocence and ignorance. "Who?"

"The woman found dead by the river a few days ago. Velia Solano could be an alias, but I'm pretty sure you know her." He pulled a small photo from his breast pocket and slid it across the desk.

Winslow leaned forward to pick it up, then studied it at length before tossing it back. "I don't know her."

"How about this one?" Caldicott passed a morgue photo of Maria Regio to the lawyer, the exit wound from the bullet that killed her marring the left side of her head.

"Obviously I knew *her*." Winslow threw the photo down in disgust. "You and your goons drove her to that, not me."

"You had a hand in it."

"She was my *client*, William."

Caldicott slammed his fist on the desk. "Who you pimped out to Judge Perry!"

Winslow jumped at the outburst but quickly regained his composure. "You have no evidence of that."

"But Velia Solano did. That's why you killed her."

"Good God!" Winslow laughed and looked about as though he might find a candid camera crew hiding among the law books and potted plants. "I don't even know who you're talking about!"

"Solano was Maria's cousin, and she knew how to do her homework. If she hadn't already dug up enough to send you to prison, she soon would. That's why you killed her."

Crossing his arms and leaning back, Winslow shook his head. "I don't know what the hell you've been smoking, but I don't have to take this intimidation."

"You sure can dish it out, though, can't you?" Caldicott leaned forward. "Give me one good reason to think I'm off base."

"Give me one solid piece of evidence to suggest you're not."

If only Solano the elder had been strangled. Unfortunately, poison was the dish of the day. "Don't worry," Caldicott said, rising. "I will."

He was already out the door when Winslow called after him, "Don't bet on it."

His team had already searched the shore, the road, and the hill where the purse was found, but he wanted another look. He didn't expect to find new evidence; he wanted to reacquaint himself with the place. So, standing at the top of the hill, the wind tousling his hair, Caldicott breathed in the smell of water and grass and of gravel baking in the noonday sun, and cleared his mind.

Five minutes passed. Ten. Twenty. Nobody drove by, nobody walked through. Caldicott stood alone in silent contemplation. If only time travel could be real. If only he could jump back to the day the body was dumped here. Dumped, not killed. Botulinum toxin might be among the most lethal of substances, but it took its time killing, several days depending on the dose. No, the murder location had been elsewhere, specifically somewhere isolated and enclosed. The autopsy revealed the poison had been inhaled, and nobody else was known to have been affected.

Where, then? Certainly not Tom and Angie Claymore's, where Solano had lived. Probably it had been someplace like his own house, well away from people. Solano had been kidnapped, held in isolation, poisoned, left to die, and dumped here by the river.

Could Jared Winslow have done that? Only with help. Winslow was a thug, but he wasn't a thief. For a thief, obtaining the poison wouldn't be too hard. A lethal inhalation dose was on the order of ten nanograms per kilogram of body weight, six hundred nanograms for

Velia Solano, practically nothing. The right medical facility would have far more in stock, and it wasn't a controlled substance.

Well, then. Case solved. Caldicott had records on most of the county's thieves, whether known or unknown. How many could have a connection to Maria Regio? Probably no more than one. Find that one, connect him to Winslow, done.

About to go, Caldicott detected a puff of musty wind escaped from an old house whose windows and doors, shuttered for a decade, had suddenly been thrust open, the same scent he had noticed the day the body was found.

Every muscle in his body went taught. He knew what that smell foretold.

"Hello again, Sergeant," Velia Solano said behind him.

Turning, Caldicott found himself face to face with a dead woman.

She was Velia Solano the elder, but not quite. She had the same face like an olive, the same dark eyes, the same cast of the mouth as Velia Solano the younger, but she looked no more than fifty. A third Velia Solano. Velia Solano the middling.

And yes, they were truly all one. He could see it in those eyes, just as Juan Garza had said. It wasn't a hoax after all.

"Who *are* you?" Caldicott asked.

She smiled, not without sympathy for his confusion. "I told you once, a few days ago, a couple of decades ago."

"Yes, but who the hell *are* you?"

She turned to the river, looked at the very spot where she would, or did, turn up dead. "Did you solve it?"

Caldicott watched her until she shot him a look of inquiry. "It's about Maria Regio, isn't it?"

She exhaled and gazed into the river. "Maria. Yes."

"She was in trouble with the law. Her lawyer Jared Winslow got her off the hook, but only by betraying her to a pervert of a judge, just like he did with two other women. When we closed in on Winslow, he threatened his clients with death should they give evidence against him. Naturally, we put some pressure on them to do just that. For Maria, caught between us and Winslow, it was too much and she killed herself. So now, you're gunning for Winslow, gathering evidence against him, planning to send him to jail." Caldicott raised an eyebrow. "Or kill him yourself, maybe?"

"I'm not a killer," she said.

"I didn't say I'd stop you. He deserves it."

Solano didn't react to that.

"I'm serious," he assured her. "I'd pop him myself, if I could get away with it."

"What else?" she asked.

"I suspect Winslow found out about you and silenced you. I can't prove it yet, but I think he had an accomplice."

"Who?"

"I don't know yet."

She sighed. "I don't have another twenty years. I'll be dead by then."

"Why does it have to be twenty years? Why not just stick around for a week or so?"

"It's hard to explain. Time travel involves paradoxes." She dug in her purse and pulled out a small silver compact, only it wasn't makeup. The device had a couple of buttons and blinking lights on the edge. She held it up. "Short version, this will take me whenever I want, but the return trip involves spacetime paths that limit how long I can stay in one place. Sometimes it's longer, sometimes it's shorter. Right now, it's short."

Caldicott held out a hand. "I'm not sure that makes sense. May I?"

"No." She tucked the device back into her purse. "I don't fully understand it myself, just like you don't know how DNA analysis works. I just follow the operating instructions. The rest is subquantum physics."

Which probably meant she was from further in the future than he would have guessed. "Is Maria Regio your cousin?"

"Yes. She got in trouble at home and escaped here. She didn't need a return path, so she could stay the rest of her life."

"Which wasn't long, as it turned out."

Solano lowered her gaze. "No. She got in trouble here, too, and had nobody to turn to for help." When she looked up, Caldicott saw mayhem in her eyes. "But at least now I know why she killed herself. I guessed Jared Winslow was part of the reason, and now you've given me the other half. How hard did you push her?"

He shoved his hands in his pockets and looked away. "Too hard, I guess. But if she had agreed to testify, it would have been a different story. I'm sorry she didn't."

"And I'm sorry I lied to you."

"About what?" When he looked back, she had a thirty-eight trained on him.

"I actually am a killer."

Caldicott put up his hands as though that would ward off bullets. Gently, he said, "You don't want to shoot me, Velia. Not yet, anyway. I haven't found out who killed you yet."

"You've given me enough to finish the work. Once you're dead, your files will be mine."

How had she known about that?

Somehow, she understood the unvoiced question. "We're in the same business, Sergeant. We dig up other people's dirt. Technically I don't have to kill you. Once I expose your perversion, you'll be finished. That would be gratifying. But putting a bullet in that twisted brain of yours will be more gratifying still."

She aimed.

"You'll never get those files," he countered. "I'm a police detective. As soon as I'm found dead, cops will swarm my house looking for answers."

"Mmm, wrong." Gun in her right hand, she patted her purse with her left. "I have the means to beat them to the punch. In fact — " Her hand slid into her purse, rummaged about, and came out with the time travel device. She glanced down at it.

Seizing upon her moment of inattention, Caldicott stepped forward and knocked her gun arm aside. He landed a punch to her gut, and when she doubled over, he kneed her in the face. She flopped backwards, dropping everything, eyes rolling up in her head.

Breathing hard, Caldicott stood over her. "Pull a gun on *me*, will you?"

Solano turned her head and coughed. Her fingers probed her stomach. "You'll…" She pitched over and tried to crawl away but collapsed. "…never be…" She grabbed a fistful of grass as though afraid of falling off the Earth.

"Safe," he finished. "Yeah, I suppose you could kill me last year." He picked up her purse, searched it, took everything that looked like future tech. There wasn't much, just the time travel device, an ultra-thin e-reader, and a gold pen that wasn't a pen. Dropping the purse, he pocketed the trio, walked to his car, and drove off.

Whatever Velia Solano did next, she wasn't going to kill him in the past.

Caldicott was never sure what became of her. Not in the remaining ten years of her life, at any rate. She didn't call for help, didn't turn up in any emergency room or clinic, never showed her face again in Jackson County. Time travel creates paradoxes, she had said. This was probably one of them.

Nor did he ever look for a thief with a connection to Maria Regio. Jared Winslow, it turned out, wasn't the murderer at all. The murderer would have been happy for Solano to take down Winslow, but Winslow wasn't her only target. She was after Caldicott, too, and maybe one or two other cops who worked with him to extract cooperation from Regio.

But Solano couldn't be allowed to kill cops.

So. A bit of study, which revealed the time device's operating instructions, then a hop back in time, a theft from a cosmetology clinic in California, another hop, a kidnapping, careful administration of the toxin to a victim locked in a barn, and a few days later Velia Solano's mission of vengeance came to a sorry end.

Caldicott felt odd as he flung Solano's purse into the grasses up the hill where he would soon find it, or had previously found it. The feeling persisted while he gave her body one last look before leaving the scene. He didn't feel guilt or remorse, he just felt odd, because he had killed a woman who was, in a sense, already dead. Was this murder? Or were they both trapped in a paradox of her design?

He couldn't say, but he knew things would change. They had to. His records, for one thing, had to go. That night he built a bonfire and burned all the paper, deleted all the computer files, and smashed Velia Solano's devices with a sledgehammer. He beat them over and over until his arms ached and he was soaked in sweat and nothing remained of them but the tiniest fragments, which he buried in the field behind the barn. As he buried them, he fantasized he was burying Jared Winslow.

Later still, long after midnight, he sat at the kitchen table, rolling between his fingers a partial bottle of botulinum toxin.

And he knew what he would do next.

Chicory

When the chicory blooms, you’re there.
When lightning splits the clouds
And thunder cracks
And rivulets flood the irises,
You’re there.
When leaves don warm colors of cool autumn
And pumpkins break out in toothy grins
As saints lend souls their guiding hands,
You’re there.
When the Child is in the manger,
And wise ones kneel,
Your joyous smile is there;
Among snow and ice, wind and dark,
Your warming hands are there.
When planting comes,
When the pollen flies—
not your favorite, I know—
Among the young shoots, you’re there.
The sun walks his rounds.
The cosmos turns.
And when the chicory blooms,
You’re there.

~ *June 18, 2023*

Thank you for reading! Please leave a short, honest review wherever you bought this book. I greatly appreciate it, and it will help others discover my books.

About the Author

Dale E. Lehman is an award-winning writer, veteran software developer, amateur astronomer, and bonsai artist in training. He principally writes mysteries, science fiction, and humor. In addition to his novels, his writing has appeared in *Sky & Telescope* and on Medium.com. He owns and operates the imprint Red Tales. He and his late wife Kathleen have five children, six grandchildren, and two feisty cats. At any given time, Dale is at work on several novels and short stories.

To learn more about Dale and his stories and to subscribe to his newsletter, visit https://www.DaleELehman.com.

www.ingramcontent.com/pod-product-compliance
Lightning Source LLC
Chambersburg PA
CBHW070358200726
48294CB00003B/967
9781958906064